Nick Storie
Book 2a
A Killer of a Detail
(formerly A Small Detail)

Nick is called because of a missing man. He went out in a boat with a mysterious woman and didn't come back.

Contents

About the Author

CD was born in Lakeland, Florida, in 1938. He is educated in genetics and botany. He has traveled over much of the world, particularly when he was in music as a rock rhythm guitarist with some well-known bands in the late sixties and early seventies. He has worked as a high steel worker and as a longshoreman, clerk, orchidist, bar owner, salvage yard manager and landscaper – among other things.

CD began writing fiction in 1984 and has more than 300 books published as of 3/15/16 in SciFi, murder, orchid culture and various other fields.

He now resides in Puerto Armuelles, David, and Gualaca, Chiriqui, Panamá, where he continues research into epiphytic plants and plays music with friends. He loves the culture of the indigenous people and counts a majority of his closer friends among that group. Several have "adopted" him as their father. He funds those he can afford through the universities where they have all excelled. "The Indios are very intelligent people, they are simply too poor (in material things and money. Culturally, they are very wealthy) to pursue higher education."

CD loves Panamá and the people, despite horrendous experiences (Free e-book; *Fading Paradise*). He plans to spend the rest of his life in the paradise that is Panamá

- Estrelita Suarez V. de Jaramillo – 3/15/2016

CD is involved in research of natural cancer cure at this time. It has proven effective in all cases, so far. It is based on a plant that has been in use for thousands of years, is safe, available, and cheap. He has studied botany, and was cured of a serious lymphoma with use of the plant, *Ambrosia peruviana*.

Information about this cure is free on the FaceBook group, Natural medicine research. CD asks only that all who try it please report on its effectiveness on that group.

A Killer of a Detail

<u>*Prologue*</u>

Al Terns laid back on his lawn chair in what little shade the tall coconut palms provided, sipped a weak vodka Collins, and watched the boats going in and out of the canal. There seemed one hell of a lot too much traffic anymore. The local community association was going to have to put lots more pressure on the county to connect the other end of the channel to the bay so half of them could go out by the back channel.

George and Mary Banks waved to him as they went by. Al waved back.

Bill Rinks went out. Someone was with him – a woman. He always went a little too fast, causing a wake. Showing off for whatever woman he was showing off for. Al couldn't really see who she was, so didn't know if she was a local. Maybe she was that Platt girl staying with the Banks. Wouldn't she be going out with them, then?

Maybe they planned to meet on one of the many barrier islands or something.

Al was a bit of a gossip. He liked to know what was going on around him and liked to exchange stories with the women at the community center. Since Elsie died, he didn't have much else to do. Even at sixty seven he supposed he could still be dating if he'd only bother to get himself into presentable shape, but it didn't really seem worth the effort. He was never what anyone could label a "ladies man" – and he really didn't care to start now! Sex always seemed more interesting to talk about than to do, with him. He was too inhibited for today's world. His father had been a lay preacher and had drummed negativity into him until he was almost married. He hadn't ever really loved Elsie in any real romantic sense, but they'd always been good friends and had liked each other honestly and sincerely. The marriage had been a very good one. It had lasted for thirty eight years, until Elsie died of colo-rectal cancer. Their only daughter was, surprisingly, quite beautiful. They were both plain.

There came Mel Sharpe and that Lorna woman who lived with him. They'd been out in Emmet's gulf boat. They knew everybody in the neighborhood, even though they lived over by Greentree Acres Estates. Mel was the golf semi-pro at Greentree and Lorna was the tennis coach. They were a lot of fun, but Al could never quite bring himself to condone their living together. He'd renounced religion long ago, but that still smacked of sin to him.

Emmet and Sandy Klaus. Sandy Klaus, for Christ's sake! If he heard one more joke about her stupid name he'd puke! They owned a little exclusive boutique in Naples and were very popular in the neighborhood. Anybody living there was popular, for one reason or another. It was the kind of snobby exclusive place where an unpopular person could be encouraged to move elsewhere very quickly. Even that Bill Rinks fellow, as insensitive as he sometimes seemed, and a drummer for one of those rock and roll and jazz bands, was liked.

Al sighed and sipped. So he was a snob.

There went Jamie Prescott. The Platt girl waved to him from the bow of the boat, so he saluted her with his Collins. It had to be someone else on Bill's boat, so he'd been wrong on that one, but who else could it be?

Jamie owned a sports shop. Everybody in the neighborhood got all kinds of things at wholesale, so he was solidly liked.

Well, the area was filled with single women and Rinks knew most of them it seemed sometimes, so she probably wasn't anyone from the neighborhood. Musicians (if one could even call a rock drummer a musician) always seemed to attract women in droves.

Al dozed lightly off and on, waking up each time a boat would go by either way, so he saw them all come back.

Except Bill Rinks.

Bill Rinks didn't come back.

Chapter one

"Are you and Janet coming out to the island?" Lt. Jim Hill asked of Det. Lt. Nathaniel "Nick" Storie when Nick came into Capt. Paddy James' office.

Jim was day head of homicide and Nick was night chief. Paddy was department head.

"We plan to come out Sunday morning. We'll spend the day. She has to be back in Orlando Sunday night.

"Am I ever glad she's gonna graduate in June!"

Janet Barnes was Nick's first really serious girlfriend. He was sure he would marry her from the first time they met on a case that took him to the college she was attending. She was six years younger than him, but that didn't much matter to either of them, in any way.

"The island" was a cabin Jim built on a piece of land he'd bought on a barrier island to the south. Jim would be married in May.

The two homicide cops, Paddy, and the fourth person in the office, Sgt. Marsha Blevins, aide and secretary to Paddy (And the one who really ran the department) were close friends as well, as co-workers.

Lt. Pat Matheny, the homicide head for the graveyard shift, was quite a bit too superficial and shifty to ever become very close to anyone. He was an aspiring politician who thought and acted like any other politician.

"Chile, she's gonna *be* gradua*t*ed!" Marsha corrected. "If'n you's a-gonner marry no collige girl, you's a-gonner hafta tryta learnta speak that there colligese!

"There's something odd going on at Royal Palm Estates. Somebody went out in a boat and didn't come back in. Some old guy's worried about it. Says the guy never stays out this late, or something."

"So? Have him contact the coast guard," Paddy suggested. "That's not anything to do with us, unless somebody else *did* come back in his boat. That would raise questions!"

"I already called them. The guy's the type whose hunches are usually on the money – which he has lots of!"

"Just give it to Pat when he comes in," Jim suggested. "He'll be impressed with almost anybody who even possibly might donate to his campaign fund."

"Oh, lord! That's right!" Paddy said, with a sigh. "That ass is running for the state senate, isn't he?"

"Lord, child, you is dense!" Marsha said. "He's running for the US senate! His future pop-in-law's a *state* senator!"

"Show's what you know!" Jim replied quickly. "His future big daddy-in-law's a state representative, not a senator, and they wanted him for attorney general, but that was a bit too far for him to stand a chance.

"I'll leave what's left of Friday in your capable hands. See you on the island tomorrow, Marsh. See you on Sunday, Nick.

"Paddy, you ought to come out to my little hideaway!

"Ciao!"

"I will *not* get into any boat! Not for *any* reason!" Paddy replied, positively. "Have a good weekend all. I'll leave it all to you two. Joan's got big plans for tonight, and I have to dress up. Stupid opera or something she knows I hate. Think it over *very* carefully before you marry that woman! If she's better educated than you, you have to live with this sort of thing. I *know*!"

"Paddy, you know perfectly well you love going places with Joan. You two are inseparable and you love it!" Marsh said, with a smirk.

"Who wouldn't?" Paddy fired back. "I only object to *which* places!"

Paddy was a huge man, both in height and breadth. He could put on a brand new, expensive, tailor-made suit, and look like he'd slept in it for three nights running. His wife was a very attractive, svelte, highly educated woman. They adored one another.

Paddy and Marsha went out, teasing at each other. Nick went to his desk.

Not much happened on that shift. A man was found dead in a motel room, but it turned out to be a coronary. A woman was hit by a drunk and killed, which was, sadly, a routine matter.

When Pat came on duty at two, Nick chatted a couple of minutes, then went home for the weekend.

"Nick, do you remember that guy who went out in a boat and didn't come back in on Friday?" Marsha asked, holding her hand over the phone about half an hour into Nick's shift on Monday. She held the phone up and said, "Three."

Nick punched line three. "Yes? Nick Storie here."

"Nick? This is Sgt. Samuel Robert Keller with the Florida State Marine Patrol. You had a report that one William Cole Rinks didn't return from a boating trip into the gulf late on Friday evening?"

"Well, we didn't get any names, but yes," Nick replied, shrugging at Marsh. "Sgt. Marsha Blevins referred the report to the coast guard. I'm assuming you're talking about the Royal Palms Estates misper?"

"Affirmative. An Albert Otto Terns made the initial missing person report." Sam Keller, in those few times Nick had spoken with him, always came off sounding like Sgt. "Just the Facts M'am" Friday. He never merely said, "Al Smith" or even "Mr. Smith." It was always "Mr. Aloysias Beltheuse Smith," or something.

"You have something?"

"A twenty foot fiberglass Harborcraft boat registered to a William Cole Rinks, one forty one East Canal, was found in the mangroves on the eastern side of a small unnamed barrier island seven point five nautical miles due south of Sanibel Island. There was some blood, human, type AB negative, found on the control console, seat cushion, and decking. It appears there had been some attempts made to remove the blood. Foul play is suspected.

"Captain James Andrew Dulin suggested that you be contacted, as Mr. Albert Terns (Wonders! He left out the middle name!) primarily reported suspicion of a crime to your department. The area of residence of the possible victim of any suspected violent criminal act lies within the jurisdiction of your department, thus you are better situated to investigate certain aspects of the case."

"I see. I'll get right on it. Please give Sgt. Blevins any information you have. I'll finish this status report and go out to Royal Palms Estates immediately."

He saw Marsha listening and grinned at her. If he took the information he'd sound like Keller for an hour after.

Marsha gave him the middle finger and started taking notes.

"Mr. Al Terns? I'm Det. Lt. Nick Storie. I'd like to ask you a few questions about the report you made Friday evening," Nick said, coming into the back yard by the canal to find Terns sitting at a white wrought iron table sipping a tall vodka Collins. He'd gone to the front door to ring the bell and had heard Terns yell to come on around back.

"Had a strong hunch!" Terns greeted. "Never am wrong in my hunches!

"Elsie, she was my late wife – died, you know. Anyhow, that's all beside the point. She always said it was just plain uncanny about my hunches. Sixth sense, she said.

"When he didn't come back in time for work I knew something was wrong. Sort of added the way that woman was wrapped up and knew there was some big trouble on the horizon! You add a sexy woman to a womanizer, it's like a match to gasoline.

"Care for some Collins, Nick? Whole pitcher there. You don't have one, I'll drink it all."

"Thanks. I'd really like one, but I'm on duty at the moment. Care to connect the dots?" If Terns was going to talk in riddles he would, too.

Didn't phase him.

"Uh-huh! I do do that! Let's see.

"The Banks went out a bit before Bill and the mystery woman. They have a twenty eight foot Sea Ray. Beautiful job!

"That was about twoish. Bill and the woman went out maybe two ten or so. He always goes a bit too fast. Wake beats our stuff up, you see. Don't like it, but what can you do?

"See, I thought maybe the Platt girl was with him, but she went out about an hour later with Jamie Prescott, who owns the sporting goods store over on Davis. Gets all our sports stuff wholesale. The whole neighborhood. The Platt girl could do a lot worse. He seems a level sort. Stable, you know? Makes pretty decent money.

"Stop me when I get off the subject. I tend to babble on and on.

"Let me see, now. I remember thinking how the girl with Rinks couldn't be the Platt girl – I can never remember her first name. Penny or Betty or something such – because there she was!

"That's why I say mystery woman. Sounds kind of mysterious.

"Mel and Lorna went out just before them in Emmet's boat. They use it a lot of the time. He's a golfer and she's tennis.

"Don't make jokes about Sandy Klaus! Please!"

"Okay," Nick said matter-of-factly. "Let's decode this.

"The Banks, who went out first? Who are they, and why did you mention them at all?"

"Because the Platt girl – Judy! Yes! That's it! – is staying with them. I wondered why she wasn't with them when they went out. That's why I thought it was probably her on Bill's boat, at first, but she went out later. With Jamie."

"They live back that way, then?" Nick pointed along the canal to the east.

"Damned county won't open up the channel-pass back there! It's already *there*! It's not like they'd have to do any major job. Maybe dig it out a few feet deeper toward the back end. It's only two hundred feet!

"Four oh three. Just this side of the bridge."

"Right. Rinks lived at one forty one, which is on the far side of the bridge. Jamie Prescott?"

"Hell of a nice guy. Lives at four fifty two, right across the street there. There's no access from that side to the canal so he keeps his boat at a private slip up just past the bridge. You saw it when you came in. Slip number's the same as his street number. Four fifty two."

"Sandy Klaus and what he has to do with it?"

"Sandy's a she. Emmet's wife. All those stupid jokes about her name near to drive me crazy! They're over in number two twelve. Other side. Keep their boat at the slips. Mel and Lorna took their boat out."

"Mel and Lorna. They're the golf and tennis people?"

"Greentree."

"You finally lost me, but I think I was doing pretty good for awhile," Nick said, with a grin.

"I like you! Got a sense of humor!" Terns poured another glass of Collins. "Mel Sharpe's the tennis pro and instructor at Greentree, and Lorna Fields is his live-in or significant other – or whatever they call a shack-up nowadays.

"They went out, they came in. All of them went out, but Bill and some woman didn't come back.

"Bill's a rock and roller. Drummer. Loose women always chase musicians. I figure she was married and her husband caught them out there. She was bundled up so nobody'd know who she was, but he was following her, or something.

"Ask me, there's two bodies out there somewhere."

"There was only one type of blood in the boat. That can't tell us much, of course. We don't even know what blood type Rinks was. It could be the woman's."

"You can check the chromosomes."

"What?" Nick asked, confused again.

"X-Y cells means it's his blood."

"Oh, certainly. If Tiny gets a sample he'll check for that kind of thing right away. Can you describe the woman who was on Rinks' boat? Size? Weight?"

"Sort of brownish hair, I believe. Had on a big hat, but I could see a bit of her hair in back. Make it medium longish. Shoulder length. Wasn't fat, but she was on the deck sort of all stretched out, so I couldn't tell really. Average height or maybe a little tall. Not what you'd call petite, but I could be wrong, there. Laying sort of bent around with those mirrored sunglasses.

"She had on bright puke green stretch slacks and a loose sort of top. She had a scarf around her hair under the hat and on the sides of her face.

"That's about it. She looked familiar enough I thought it was the Platt girl, but that mainly means she was average.

"Come to think of it, now, the Platt girl's hair's more that reddish blonde, so I should have known. Didn't register 'til right now.

"Sure you won't have a short one?"

"No. I have to work until two. I'll get back if I need anything else."

"That walk-in medical clinic over on East Davis!" Terns cried, suddenly.

"What?" Nick was lost again.

"Bill had that Oriental flu bug going around so much a month or so back and thought he had encephalitis. He went to the clinic. They'll have his blood type!"

"That's certainly a help. I'll radio that in on my way on to Jamie Prescott's. He's right across the street there?"

"Yep! Drop in anytime you're around! I like to talk."

Nick saluted and headed for his car.

"Mr. Prescott, I hate to bother you like this, but we're afraid there's been foul play concerning a close neighbor." Nick apologized, after introducing himself. "Mr. Rinks went out on his boat Friday afternoon and never came back in, as you may have already heard. The Marine Patrol found his boat had drifted up among the mangroves. There's blood in it. There's no sign, either of Bill Rinks or of the unidentified woman who was seen on his boat with him early Friday afternoon.

"We've been told you were out in the gulf Friday. Did you see Rinks anywhere?"

"Yes. We saw him down to the south. It was about four, I think. I was fishing off the port side, so I saw them go by when Judy waved. I didn't pay too much attention to them, really."

"We're trying to identify the woman who was with him. We don't know if she's been reported as missing anywhere."

"She was a tall woman with a pretty good figure is all I know. She had on a two-piece sunbathing suit, not quite a bikini, but just a little more. She had on one of those big floppy straw Jamaican hats and mirrored sunglasses.

"I only saw her for a few seconds. I wasn't paying any particular attention to them and they passed off a ways to our starboard, so Judy might have seen them better."

"You say it was south?" Nick asked, writing each little detail down. He never knew what might prove important, but the fact that the woman had shed the "green stretch slacks" and "loose top" could prove very important. His list of items found in the boat didn't contain any such things. It didn't contain any items that a woman would carry more than a man – of any kind.

"It was about two miles before the ten thousand islands and maybe half a mile offshore. We were trying to catch spotted trout in the shallows. We didn't have much luck."

Nick asked a few more questions, then went out. The Banks and Judy Platt were probably his next best witnesses. It was possible Judy saw something that would identify the woman.

They weren't home, so he went to see Emmet and Sandy Klaus.

"Then you will often lend your boat to Sharpe – or anyone?" Nick asked.

"Yes. A couple of times a month," Emmet answered. "I get free golf advice and Sandy gets tennis instructions. Sandy and I went to the Medieval Pageant in Ft. Myers, so we didn't plan to use it."

"Would you care for a hot, or cold, cup of coffee,

Lieutenant?" Sandy asked. "I've got a fresh pot."

She was a comfortable, slightly plump woman in her forties, about the same age as her husband. She had mousy brown hair while Emmet only had a fringe of salt-and-pepper hair. Both wore steel rimmed glasses. Emmet, at five ten, was a couple of inches taller than Sandy.

"Lorna and Mel are popular around the area," Emmet continued. "They do favors for us and we do favors for them."

"Thank you, I would really appreciate a hot cup," Nick replied to Sandy. "Black, please," then to Emmet, "What I have to know is if they saw anything out there Friday afternoon."

"Isn't it just terrible?" Sandy said, handing Nick a large mug of very good coffee. "Bill was always a lot of fun. I just can't believe he...." she shuddered.

"He was a jazz musician," Emmet said. "He ran around with a bunch of groupies. I don't think he used drugs – except maybe marijuana sometimes – or any of that, but he couldn't keep his pants zipped.

"He started in New Orleans, which is where his first band was from. You may've heard of them, `The Wonknight Stand?' Whole bunch were in trouble all the time. Zipper trouble, mostly. Somebody killed one of them in a brawl in a bar over some cheap whore."

"Em!" Sandy exclaimed.

"We can't be nice and follow polite conventions, Hon," Emmet pointed out. "I can see they don't believe Bill met with any accident out there.

"Lieutenant, was he murdered?"

"We don't know what happened to him. The Marine Patrol found his boat, and there was quite a lot of blood in it. It could be his or it could be the woman's who was with him or it could be a third person's. There might have been some kind of accident. He might have cut himself or any number of things, but we don't think so. We do suspect foul play, quite frankly, but we don't know if he was the victim or the perpetrator."

"Oh, boy! You really *do* use those kinds of words! " Sandy cried.

"Me? You should hear Sam Keller!" Nick grinned. "`Just the facts, M'am! Did you directly witness the alleged criminal act of jaywalking perpetrated by Mr. Alexius Peter Cadwalader Forthhampton Julianus Reginald Braithewaite the Fourth on the afternoon of August the eleventh at precisely three seventeen PM at the north corner of Fifth Avenue and Third Street in the northwest lane at which time the aforementioned individual allegedly deliberately and with malice aforethought stepped approximately four and three tenths of an inch outside of the clearly marked pedestrian lane?'"

"You're kidding!" She grinned back.

"Not much. I talked to him for about five minutes earlier today and still catch myself using that kind of language. Perpetrator *is* a word I use, though.

"Tiny, the coroner, will be doing a chromosome check to see if the blood's male or female and we're checking to see if it was Rinks' blood type. We have to know who that woman with him was."

"So. You suspect her?" Emmet asked, looking shrewdly at Nick.

"There's absolutely nothing on that boat to indicate she was ever on it. When she went out, she was wearing slacks. When they were later seen out in the gulf she was wearing a bathing suit. The slacks would logically still be in the boat unless she, or someone else, removed them, deliberately.

"Deliberately removing those items is a little detail that

shows us either she or someone else was trying to guarantee she wasn't identified as having been the one on the boat. If it was her, she did something to Rinks, and if it was someone else, she probably had something done to her. That, or she can identify whoever did whatever."

"You take on speech habits of people, don't you?" Sandy asked. "You've been talking to Al Terns."

"That obvious, huh?" He grinned.

"If you can follow him, he usually has a lot to say," Emmet said. "There's not too much that goes on around here he doesn't know about."

"He's the local village gossip, but he's never vicious with it," Sandy explained. "He drinks all day every day and talks on and on. He's never really drunk."

"He's become immune to the stuff," Emmet suggested. "I think we'd find him strange if he didn't have a few."

"He's found the formula to stay at a pleasant glow," Nick said. "The bottle only had a little bit missing and he had an almost full pitcher, so he's got it figured to about a third of a shot per glass.

"He drinks about one glass every half hour, so that's about one beer per hour in alcohol. He never really gets drunk, but his liver's on overtime if he's been doing it long."

"We've known him about nine years," Sandy agreed. "Even when Elsie was alive he was like that."

"His wife? What did she die of?"

"Female and colon cancer that spread all over," Emmet answered. "They have a daughter. Truly beautiful girl. She lives up north somewhere."

"It's really amazing how two people like Al and Elsie could have such a striking beauty for a daughter," Sandy said. "Elsie was even plainer than Al."

"I think Bill probably dated her the last time she was

here," Emmet replied. "I know Al was torn. He liked Bill, but he frowns on all pop musicians on general principles. His father was a religious fanatic, and, even though Al professes to not be religious, he still tends to judge people."

"Any specific things?" Nick asked, perking up.

"No, not really. They went out a few times," Sandy replied. "She sings. She sang for his jazz band sometimes, but lots of his girlfriends do. I think Al disapproved of the fact Rinks ever *had* all those girlfriends, more than anything else."

"Lorna Fields sang with them a few times when they played at the country club," Emmet said. "Even June.

"Well, June tried, anyhow, when they played at her place. She doesn't have much talent, I'm afraid. Lorna's pretty fair."

"June?"

"June Cerf," Sandy answered. "She owns Cerf's Surf Lounge. It's a nightclub and restaurant. She lives the next block down from here."

"Did Rinks date her?"

"Lord above, no way!" Sandy laughed. "She only dates rich old multimillionaires! She's engaged to that Hodgkinson man who owns all that land east of Bonita and on down south. He's maybe seventy five and she's about thirty three. You can ask Al about it. He says they'd already be married if she'd agree to sign a prenuptial.

"She says she has lots of property, too, and the restaurant. She'd be a total fool to sign any kind of agreement that would leave him everything if anything happened to her and her nothing if anything happened to him.

"He had a private detective following her once and she broke it off until he apologized and swore he wouldn't ever do that again. I suppose a seventy year old man dating a thirty year old woman has plenty to be suspicious or jealous about.

"We don't have much to gossip about around here, but what we have is juicy!

"June was supposed to go to the pageant with us, but she was called in for some emergency at the restaurant. She's really nice enough, but she's looking out strictly for number one."

"Hon, you let Al spread the gossip," Emmet cautioned. "It's mostly a bunch of hearsay. We don't *know* any of it!"

"Al Tern's never been far wrong, that I know of!" she returned, defensively. "I'm not saying anything she wouldn't admit about herself!"

Nick changed the subject. "Did Rinks ever date Lorna, or did she just sing for his band?"

"Lorna? No, she wouldn't date anyone," Sandy said. "She and Mel are too tight."

They chatted awhile, then Nick left. He drove by the Banks' to find there was still no one there.

Cerf's Surf Restaurant and Lounge, live entertainment, was only two blocks off the route back to the station, so he stopped and went in. He asked to speak with Miss June Cerf and was shown into a rather spacious and somewhat ostentatious office by the bartender, who didn't have anyone but several people working on the stage in the place. He explained the entertainment lounge was closed on Monday nights because they just had a little comedy show in the restaurant section.

Judy Cerf was a very poised, highly confident, attractive woman with reddish brown hair, startling green eyes, an exceptional figure, and a low pleasant voice. She was tall, almost six feet.

"Lt. Storie? What's the problem now? The band too loud for the bowling alley crowd?" she asked, with a dazzling smile.

"No, not that I'm aware of." Nick returned the smile. "I'm with homicide. Bill Rinks, one of your neighbors, is feared dead of foul play. We understand his band played here from time to time.

"Was there ever any kind of incident? A jealous husband or boyfriend who acted angry?"

"Bill? He doesn't have any band. He's drummer for The Gathering C, a sometimes jazz band. They've played here every two months for perhaps three years. He plays studio for rock and jazz and subs for any band who needs a really professional drummer. He's good."

"Sometimes band?"

"Jazz doesn't pay a decent living, so they booked our cycle and another club's on rotation basis. Between those two weeks every two months the guys can farm out their backup services. They're all good enough that they make plenty. The jazz is more a hobby than a business. They were supposed to play here this week, but Stinger canceled. They got a project that pays a lot more, so they'd traded gigs with The Stranglers out there setting up now. They're to play next week, but without Bill....

"You say you think he's dead?"

Nick explained about the boat and the blood.

"I really don't see anyone wanting to kill him, unless maybe it *was* a boyfriend. It certainly wasn't any angry husband. Bill didn't do windows or married women.

"That's an inside line. We get a lot of guys like Bill, and a lot who don't care if the woman's married or not. Bill did care.

"I don't think he spent many nights alone judging by what I've seen so far."

Nick thanked her and went out front to the lounge area, where the bartender was washing glasses and watching the band put duct tape all over the stage.

"I think they use about ten rolls of that crap every time they set up," the bartender said. "All the bands do."

"Yeah. Part of the business, I guess. Have to tie down all those cords."

"Yeah, and I have to clean up after them!"

"If this section's closed Mondays, why have a bartender?"

"Restock, set up, keep an eye on the people in and out and make cocktails for the restaurant. I'm Len, by the way.

"What're we in for today? Complaints about the noise, or the church bitching because we sell demon rum at all?"

"No. I'm working on a murder case." A bored waitress came in a side door to hand Len a slip of paper. He dropped four glasses onto her tray and quickly made two perfect Manhattans and two Old Fashioneds, punched on the cash register, took the money from a twenty she handed him, and dropped the change on her tray.

"They pay the bar separately," Len said, coming back to sit a cup of coffee in front of Nick. He poured one himself. "Stinking system. I don't get any tips, but June pays extra for Monday.

"You got a few minutes to talk? I go bugs out here.

"What's this place got to do with any murder?"

"It's not definite there's been any murder, but we think Bill Rinks is dead. We found his boat and a lot of blood. He never came home. Miss Cerf's a neighbor, and he played in a band here. We needed to know if anyone saw or heard anything to give us a direction. Bill was quite the man for the ladies, or so I've heard."

"Bill? Aw, no! Bill's a nice guy! Really?

"He was what you call discriminating, with the women. They liked him because he was so sensitive – and it didn't hurt he looked like that tennis pro guy, Agassi! He treated all of them like he respected them. They eat that stuff up.

"I'm sorry to hear that. I hope like hell you're wrong.

"Some guy in a band he was with in New Orleans was murdered. That happened right in the middle of June's Place.

"They were supposed to play here this week."

"So Miss Cerf informs me. They canceled, and she had to come in Friday afternoon to book these guys?

"June's Place?"

"I guess she came in for that, too. She came in for something – in a hell of a lousy mood. I sort of wondered why they traded gigs. Barney, he's sax man and leader of the Stranglers – the fat one – said they traded bookings on Thursday so Stinger – the keyboard man with The Gathering C – called him up late and said they were booked for a prob three straight at New Jazz Gems.

"Miss Cerf had a cheap little club out towards the lake in New Orleans. She inherited it. It was one of those mixed rough beer and wine taverns, but she got enough for it to get out and move down here. The clientele were the kinds who brawled a lot."

"I don't understand a lot of those musician's terms. What does that stuff about the band mean?"

"Three straight's three straight days booked and New Jazz Gems is a studio," Len answered, looking around and pouring a dash of Kahlua into his own and Nick's coffee, then slipping the bottle back under the counter. "June'd raise hell if she knew I did that, okay?"

Nick grinned and nodded.

"Anyhow. New Jazz Gems is a local recording studio. Some big blow's in town and wants to jam cut a couple spontaneous. The Gathering's known all over for their jam work, so they'd make a sixer or eighter. They'll do that sometimes. We just swing our cycle.

"Now I'll translate.

"A local recording studio called The Gathering C and offered them six or eight times what they'd make here in a week to play jam improv behind a big known star for three nights. Stinger called in and June booked The Stranglers in their place, so they'd play The Stranglers' gig here next month."

"Happen much?"

"Sometimes. Maybe once a year or so. It's part of the business."

"So then Miss Cerf had to change her plans for Friday. That would be why she didn't go to Ft. Myers with Sandy and Emmet Klaus. She had to be here."

"Yeah, I guess. She gets in that office and sorta camps sometimes. You were in there, so you know it's a lot like a luxury condo."

"Hah! If I had a place like that to stay I'd never go home!"

"Me neither. She even stays in there sometimes overnight ... when business is ... I should learn when to keep my mouth shut!"

"I hear her ancient lover even has a private detective checking on her. You didn't hear me say that, either!

"I suppose she would try to find some entertainment on the side, now and then. I can't see any seventy year old handling a woman like that. I can't see many guys *my* age handling it!"

"She's discreet, you know." He said with a relieved grin. "Sometimes, when the pressure's building up too much, she has a long late night business conference with somebody. She's usually pure hell on wheels for a couple days afterward. Scared we'll blab, or something.

"When something's not going right she locks herself inside that office. We know better than to bother her."

"She could lock the office and sneak out back," Nick suggested, thoughtfully. "Her boyfriend's private detective would never know she was gone. Neither would you."

"Oh, we'd know all right!" he argued, and went to take an order from another waitress. He made six drinks, made the change and came back.

"How would you know? All you'd know is she went in and locked the door."

"When she's in that kind of bad mood she uses the inside phone to bitch about everything all the time." He grinned. "It's not like she does it much, but when something goes wrong. We wait her out and she apologizes when she gets over it."

"So you know for a fact she was in there Friday. That gives her an alibi, if she needs one."

"Friday she fired Connie, then hired her back – Connie's the cute redheaded waitress that came in right after you stopped. She called me and said it was my ass if she saw spots on the glasses that night. She called later to say I'd screwed up the mix order and she'd have to spend the whole damned day trying to keep the damned business out of bankruptcy. She called about eight to apologize about that because she read a two-case order as a twenty-case order or something such.

"She was in there, alright, and a lot worse than usual! The inside phones were sizzling for awhile!"

Two waitresses came in at once. Nick thanked him, tossed down the coffee, and left.

Greentree was out on the Trail East. It wasn't too far, so Nick went right instead of left out of the restaurant. He'd take a chance Mel Sharpe and Lorna Fields would be there. He might as well get all the background done, in case he even had a case. A radio check showed it was a quiet night at the station, but that was normal since the tourist season was over.

The country club was one of those overdone things so common in the area. Janet would cringe and call it "Tourist Tacky" from something she'd read by John D. MacDonald. It did look like a cheap imitation of a cheap imitation to Nick.

Mel wasn't around, but Lorna was on the back courts, so he watched her play and instruct for twenty minutes, then went to ask if he could have just a few minutes.

"Sure! I'm all done for tonight!" she replied. "Come on into my office, okay? I have to get out of these things."

He followed her into a nice office, where she took off her shoes and socks and went into a frosted glass door to a shower.

"Sandy called me and told me about Bill," she said, tossing her shorts and shirt over the door. They were followed by the undergarments and the sound of the shower.

"I have to learn everything anyone knows while it's fresh. We don't know for certain we have a case, but I think we do. Al Terns said you and Mel were out in Emmet's boat, so you might have seen them out there somewhere.

"Did you?"

"We passed them at the outer channel marker. They turned south and we went on out."

"What can you tell me about the woman with him?"

"She was laying on the bow decking in green tights and a big floppy Jamaican straw hat." She turned off the shower. "She was talking on the phone. Bill waved and we waved back. I didn't pay too much attention to her. Mel probably didn't even see her from down there. He was inside and I was up on the cabin. He doesn't like to drive from the flying bridge when it's choppy like that.

"Do you play tennis?"

"Noy much. No golf either. I like swimming and scuba diving and volleyball. Water skiing's fun."

"Beach and water. You've got a pretty good build for tennis and basketball. You're quick.

"Which one of us knocked Bill off?"

Nick grinned as she stepped out of the shower stall with a towel partly covering her. "Oh, that! We believe Mel killed him in a fit of jealous rage because of your affair with him."

"In my wildest dreams!" she answered, with an impish leer. "He was really a dream stud. Looked like Andy A, so any tennis broad would naturally flip. Trouble was, *Bill* wouldn't play those idiotic games, because he considered me and Mel as a couple. If I would've made it with him, Mel would just consider it a license for him to make it with some other broad. We're pretty realistic about that sort of thing – which is why I'd flirt and tease, but never actually do anything. Mel wouldn't either. I might've with Bill. I think he'd be worth it."

"You say the woman was talking on a phone? On the boat?"

"Oh, sure! Lots of people take their cellulars out or use SS." She slipped a dress over her head, letting the towel drop at the same time. Nick looked away, which amused her. "I call on the SS on Sandy's boat all the time."

"I see. You only saw them that once?"

"Uh-huh. We went on out and did some grouper fishing off the six mile reef. We're having the catch for supper. Mel's cooking it now. Care to join us?"

"I'm on duty. I have to get back. Thanks."

"Learn anything?" Pat Matheny asked as he checked in as Nick checked out. "I hear you have a little case to fill the dreary hours."

"I might have a case. I think I have. So far, I have nothing. Not even a vague suspect, but then, I don't have a body or anything, either."

"Tiny left a note here for you," Pat said. "It's there on my desk. Par for the course."

Nick took the note. The blood in the boat was male and the clinic confirmed it was Rinks' type. That was exactly what Nick expected.

<u>*Chapter two*</u>

"I called you to come in early today because you now have a case," Paddy said Tuesday morning about ten in his office. "You always do work days when you have something. I know you've already put a lot of the background together. I read your files.

"Marsha, you took that report. You tell Nick about it, then we can have a little conference."

"The deceased body of one William Cole Rinks was discovered at approximately eight fifteen this morning tangled among the roots of red mangroves in the mouth of Parson's Creek where it meets Otter Run Bay four tenths of a mile south by southeast of Kimmins Point, at which the fiberglass Harborcra...." Marsha began.

"Knock it off!" Nick demanded. "So Sam Keller called you to say they found Rinks' body."

She grinned at Nick, and continued, "He'd been shot once in the back and once in the upper left side with a twenty five automatic. The second one killed him.

"That's about what a report almost twelve minutes long actually said.

"I vote we let Paddy take the next call from Keller!"

"Yeah, right," Paddy replied, as Jim came in. "Jim, you've read Nick's report on Rinks. Any suggestions?"

"Can Terns prove he was there in that lawn chair from about three o'clock, when the last boat he mentioned went out, and five thirty, when the first of them came back in? Was he really upset far more than he let on about Rinks dating his daughter? Does he even realize that Rinks, if he dated her, slept with her as well, and how does he react?"

"I have to check on that," Nick said. "Can Mel and Lorna prove they went on out and that they didn't follow Rinks?

Did Rinks ever actually make it with Lorna?"

"And can Jamie Prescott and Judy Platt prove they didn't follow them?" Marsha asked. "Did Rinks make it with Judy, who Prescott considers his own girl?"

"You'll still have to interview the Banks and Miss Platt," Paddy pointed out. "What about them? Was Rinks messing with Miss Platt? Did they disapprove?"

"Is there any way the Cerf woman can prove she was actually in her office?" Jim asked. "Was he ever one of her special `business conferences' the bartender mentioned?"

"If they don't find a woman's body, who was the woman on his boat?" Marsha asked. "Did some other musician have any reason to want to get rid of Rinks?"

"How many boyfriends did Rinks get in bad with through his womanizing?" Nick asked. "I think I have enough background to keep busy on today. First off, I have to see Judy Platt and the Banks. Maybe that alone will eliminate some of them."

"Do you have any hunches?" Jim asked.

"Just a couple of maybe's," Nick answered. "They're pretty weak, but it's something I can check, I think.

"You noticed the woman was using a phone out there?"

"Oh, yeah! If it was ship to shore the phone company should have records," Marsha said.

"If it was cellular and was one of your suspects they'll also be in the carrier records," Paddy pointed out. "You should be able to trace that, at least."

"If it was boosted cellular, the calls will be reported from the nearest pickup, probably on an island like where my place is," Jim suggested.

"If any of them have a cellular phone I can locate time and duration of the calls and the nearest pickup tower," Nick agreed. "That'll put it right smack dab in someone's lap!

"If it's not one of my suspects, I'm in trouble. I can check on all calls from the general area."

"Interview that Platt woman and the Banks, first," Paddy said. "Jim, there's a domestic abuse thing out the trail you'll have to investigate. It got messy to the degree it might turn into M one.

"Marsha, get Commissioner Morgen on the phone for me, then I'll contact Judge Collins and get a court order for you to see the records of the phone company, Nick. It'll be on your desk later.

"Well? Get cracking! You're not among the most highly paid government employees in the entire state to be standing around this office!"

Nick and Jim saluted him with their middle fingers, grinned, and went out. Nick sat at his desk to read the report on Rinks, then headed for the Banks home.

"I'm glad I finally caught you," Nick said to Mary Banks. "I have to ask you a few questions about Friday afternoon.

"Is your husband or Miss Judy Platt around?"

"They went out fishing, but they'll be back in a half hour. We're going to the new boat show this afternoon. In Ft. Meyers.

"Is it about poor Bill Rinks? Have they learned anything yet?"

"Yes, I'm afraid so. The MP found his body this morning, not far from where they found his boat. He was most definitely murdered.

"According to Al Terns you went out about the same time Rinks did. Did you see him anywhere?"

"Well, no, not that I recall. We just went out the channel and north to New Pass, where we met the Ed Gardeners and shared a picnic. They live over in Bonita Springs and have use of the island. We had the picnic and visited until around a quarter to five, then we came back in.

"Those people using the Klaus' boat were a little ahead of us. They came in from the reef and showed us two grouper they caught."

"Did Miss Platt mention having seen Rinks out there to you?"

"Oh, yes! When we heard he was missing she said he was out south with some girl. She said they went by no more than a hundred feet away and the girl seemed angry about something. She was yelling into a phone.

"She wasn't yelling at Bill. She was mad at someone on the phone. Judy didn't hear much, but she said it sounded like she was really telling off a boyfriend or something."

"I see. Miss Platt didn't recognize the woman?"

"She said she was tall, but she had on a big hat and a scarf around her face and was wearing gloves."

"Gloves?! And that didn't make Miss Platt suspicious?"

"Suspicious? Why, no. Why would it?" she asked, looking at him strangely.

"But why would anyone in a bathing suit wear gloves?"

"She had light skin. She wanted to protect it from the sun. A lot of women cover their face and hands in the sun. The skin ages very fast from sun damage on the face, particularly, and on the hands. The rest of the body doesn't show it nearly so much. I wear gloves if I'm going to be out for long. I also wear a wide hat and sunglasses in the sun. Women have been wearing gloves and big hats for centuries for that same reason. That's why women gardeners are always depicted in hats and gloves, as well as all the women on those safaris and old western things."

"I never thought of that point, but you're right!" Nick exclaimed. "I've never once wondered why ... I thought the gloves were to keep dirt off, but the pictures always showed the women picking flowers or herbs. I'll be damned! My own girlfriend wore gloves when we went fishing on Sunday. I never thought about it.

"I'll be damned! You live and learn!"

"Men aren't very observant of women's hands. They tend to look at legs and bosoms.

"I hear the boat coming in. George always honks three short blasts to tell me I can get the lunch on the table. You can ask Judy about seeing them, but break it to her about them finding Bill's body as easily as you can. She was a little sweet on him."

Nick nodded and went to the dock down by the bridge, where Judy Platt was standing on the dock, looping the bow line around a tie-down peg. She looked up and smiled. Nick couldn't help noticing she was more than average good looking.

"Miss Platt? I'm Lt. Nick Storie. May I ask you a few questions?"

"About Bill? Have they found him?"

"I'm afraid so."

"Oh, no! If you say it that way ... he's dead?" she asked, shock evident on her face. "Give me a minute? I expected it, but I did hope...."

"I'm sorry. Everyone seems to have liked him. I'll ask Mr. Banks a couple of questions first."

"You will? What's going on?" George asked, coming from the stern line.

"I'm Det. Lt. Nick Storie from Naples South Station, Homicide," Nick introduced, offering his hand. "I'm here investigating the murder of Bill Rinks.

"I've spoken with your wife and she didn't remember seeing Mr. Rinks Friday. Did you?"

"No. We went on up north to New Pass. Judy saw him, though. Some woman was with him.

"So he was murdered? You know that for sure?"

"I'm afraid so. His body was found earlier this morning. We're trying to find who the woman was who was out there in that boat with him."

"Hmm. Could'a been almost anybody. He didn't stick with any one more than a day. Beats me why they didn't seem to care!"

"Oh, Uncle George!" Judy said. "Bill never pretended he was in love or even interested in anything steady. We dated several times, not only once.

"Mr. Storie, he didn't mark up his conquests on some kind of list or other, he only dated women he could respect. He was interested in people as people and he'd do anything he could to help anybody who needed him. He was somebody anyone could just *talk* with about absolutely anything. He really understood. It wasn't an act. We didn't compete for him – because it wouldn't do any good, and we knew it."

"I'm beginning to see. I'm not beginning to understand it, yet, but I don't understand my own fiancee, so I surely couldn't understand anyone else.

"Mrs. Banks said you told her that the woman seemed to be having an argument with someone on the phone?"

"It sounded like it. She was yelling about something, but I couldn't hear any of the words. Our motor was too loud. It was more the way she was waving her arm around and the tone that made me think probably she was having a fight with a boyfrien.... Oh! Dear God! She might have been telling some lunatic boyfriend she was out there with Bill! Oh, my God!"

"We'll have to find out everything we can about that one. Can you describe her?"

"I couldn't see anything except for her shape. She was tall and very, what you'd call statuesque. Fair skin."

"Well, every little bit helps. If you can think of anything

else at all, call me, please?" He gave her a card. She nodded.

"I suppose I'll call on Terns again while I'm out here."

"If anyone knows anything, he's it!" George agreed. "Not much gets past him."

"He said he saw you go out and come in." Nick grinned. "He saw everyone go out and come in – except Bill didn't come in, so he called in the missing persons report that got us into it early.

"Do either of you know definitely the names of any girls Bill was dating?"

"Cetainly. There was Amy Fletcher," Judy answered. "She was more serious than he liked, but they'd worked it out, I'm sure. She lives in Parkwood Dream Condos, but I don't know which one."

"OK. I'll find her. I guess I'll stop by at Al's first."

"Al's really sweet," Judy said. "Tell him hello for me."

Nick chatted a minute, then headed for Al's.

"Ah! Still on duty?" Al greeted. "If not, pour yourself a tall one! They're not too strong.

"Hear they found Rinks. Shot full of holes. (Damn it! Now I can't use the old, `Ahha! And how did *you* know he was shot, huh!?' routine, Nick thought.) Haven't found the woman.

"There'll be bunch of women who'll cry over him, I suppose.

"Know who the woman was yet?"

"Not even maybe perhaps. I've been thinking about some things you might be able to help with, assuming you didn't go out there and plug him yourself."

"Me? Why would I do that? I'm very flattered you think I'd have the nerve to shoot somebody – I think – but why me?"

"Why not? I have to suspect everyone in the state I wasn't with the whole afternoon on Friday. He'd dated your daughter, and you certainly would never approve of that. No father would."

"He probably slept with her, far as that goes. A father wants his daughter to be pure until she gets married. I've asked a couple of girls I know have slept with him why they didn't seem to get pissed because he slept with everybody. They all said it wasn't that way with Bill.

"What the hell is that supposed to mean? In my day, a woman only slept with a man after she was guaranteed they'd get married! Now they sleep with some Bill Rinks because he's so understanding and sweet? Excuse my ass if that's 'way too modern for me! Damned pill was the worst thing ever happened to this world! Girls asked *him* to bed them! They figured he was doing *them* the favor!

"I waved to everybody who went in or out, so I was here. Doc and Frannie were pan fishing over on their dock next door all afternoon. We hollered at each other every once in awhile. Doc came over for a drink, once. No way I could've gone out. My boat never left the dock last Friday. That's another thing.

"Don't have any idea who she was?"

"The woman, seen by umpty dozen people on the boat, but who nobody, so far, can describe, beyond that she's tall and has a good figure? No. We know very little about that one.

"Know any names you can give me of the girls who slept with him, then didn't care that he slept around?"

"She shot him full of holes. She went out all wrapped up so nobody'd know who she was. She'd planned to shoot him all along. There has to be some big reason for that."

"She wasn't still on the boat and she didn't leave so much as a single fingerprint on it," Nick agreed. "That means she had to have gotten off of it sometime after Miss Platt and Mr. Prescott saw him.

"Did someone meet her out there or did she go to land – and how? I should be asking Judy and Jamie who else they saw down there.

"There has to be a motive, too. I'll have to dig for that. I'll have to check several things I have already."

"Hmm, Well there was Rita Gomez, sort of fiery type, and has a way to look that makes you wonder if she's as hot as her eyes, if you get the drift. She claimed she wouldn't be bothered if he slept around because a woman would have to expect that in such a man.,Her and a Kitty Something-or-other both told me the very same thing. It sort of shocked me at the time, but that's the way they live today."

"Do you know where those two girls live?"

"Rita lives over the canal in that pink stucco house. He topped off his glass. "Kitty's from New Jersey and went back up about three months ago. Couldn't find work here."

"I'll have to call on Rita Gomez, I suppose."

"You have an idea who did it, don't you?" Al asked, giving Nick the shrewd look again. "Some woman."

"Within a few possibilities, I think just maybe I do. It's a matter of tying up loose details. The killer made some pretty stupid mistakes – or else the killer's deliberately leaving trails that lead nowhere.

"This one's a puzzle. I can't find the damned motive."

"Unless someone's lying."

"The trouble with that comes down to nobody lying or most of them lying. I can't see any motive for the ones I think might have done it."

"You have a good idea who it was."

"I know who I personally *think* did it, but I don't dare concentrate on that one because it's too easy to be wrong.

If I waste a lot of my time on the wrong suspect I'll lose the real killer."

"The only thing I can suggest is to have another drink!" Al happily poured one for himself.

"How can I get in touch with your daughter?" Nick asked. He was somewhat surprised when Al grinned broadly and gave him the address and phone number.

"Miss Platt, I have to check on one more thing while I'm out here. I have to know if you recognised anyone else from around here immediately before or anytime after you saw Rinks down by the Ten Thousand Islands?"

"Please call me Judy," she answered, thinking deeply. "Let me try to picture it. There were four or five other boats in the area, but none of them seemed familiar, in any particular way. One was a big blue and white cabin job, two of ... no, three ... were eighteen or twenty footers. Those walkthroughs, like Jamie's. Not the cabin.... There were two boats, little Johnboats, on the pieces of shell beach. I saw them through the binoculars. Two families were having a picnic. Two men, two women and three children. I saw a small aluminum boat, maybe a twelve footer, with one of those little ten or fifteen horse outboards on it anchored just inside the bay. `Diver down' flags around it, so people would give it a good wide berth in that shallow water. The divers couldn't go deep enough to avoid your prop.

"No. I'm afraid there was no one from around here but Jamie and me and Bill and that woman. There were several commercial fishermen. Two boats, I think. They're always out around those shallows."

"What? Crabbers? Gillnetters?"

"Gillnetters. Mullet fishermen. One in a green boat with one of those lights on a boom and one white boat with the console in the middle. One of those things that look like they're rearing out of the water in front."

"What are you looking for?" George Banks asked. "You thought of something or Al said something for you to come back."

"The woman has never been found, so either her body's somewhere out there or someone took her off Bill's boat. Add to that, the killer, if it wasn't the woman, had to get out there, somehow."

"Why does it have to be someone from right around here?" Mary Banks asked.

"It doesn't, but ninety five percent of the murders I've investigated were committed by someone familiar with the victim, usually family or close friend. This kind of murder demands a solid motive. It wasn't some random violence thing."

"I don't know," Mary said. "You read in the papers all the time about maniacs. Somebody could have killed Bill and raped the woman with him."

"Those kinds of murders usually come in a definite series. The woman had a phone, so she would have called nine one one or something as soon as they were attacked, even if she knew the attacker.

"I'm wondering about that cell phone! Would whoever she was talking to hear the boat?"

"But! That means she killed Bill! There's no other...!" Judy cried.

"The cell phones have a damper on the mouthpiece. They don't pick up traffic noises," George said. "I guess she did have to be the killer, didn't she?"

"It's more than fifty-fifty." Nick asked a few more questions, then headed for the next street and Rita Gomez. She wasn't home today, but a maid at told him she was at the community center, so he headed there.

"Miss Gomez, I have a few questions. It's about Bill Rinks," Nick said, after introducing himself.

Rita was tall and attractive, with an exceptional figure and long dark auburn hair. Nick could see what Al meant about her eyes.

"I cried myself to sleep about Bill," she replied. "He was a wonderful man. I wanted more than anything in life to be the special one to him."

"He wasn't the kind to be faithful to one woman," Nick replied, watching her carefully.

"Verdad. It would not be fair for any woman to ask that he be a one woman man. Bill, he was, how you say?, the dream of a man. He had such fire and passion, but he was so, so ... honest. It mattered true to him about me, about the others. We were not only just another woman he used and threw away. He cared."

"For all of you?"

"Si. It is so sad there is no other man in the whole world who is like he was." Tears started at the corners of her eyes. "He could love truly all he loved, but he could never be in love. Do you understand?"

"No. I've never known anyone like he seems to have been.

"You were in love with him?"

"Oh, si! Es cierto! We all were in love with him."

"You understand that I have to ask you where you were last Friday afternoon and evening?"

"I was here, at home, or shopping, at the beach – who knows? I was everywhere. I could kill myself for Bill, but I could never kill him!"

"That seems to be the general consensus," Nick replied, dryly. "Somebody *did* kill him."

"Sorry to bother you, but I have to ask you a question or

two," Nick said, looking around J. T. Prescott's Sportsman Supplies. "It's about the Rinks murder.

"Did you see anyone down in the Ten Thousand Islands area who was familiar, in any way – other than Rinks?"

"Just Ted and Carla ... no, that was way north when we were on the way in," Jamie replied. "Not that I can recall.

"Lieutenant, have you checked with the phone company? That woman was using a phone, so there's SS or boosted cellular. Bill didn't have either on his boat, so it'll be in the woman's name – and there are records."

"Oh? Did you make any calls from out in the gulf?"

He got a grin back. "CB. No phone or SS."

"There are a lot of CB messages back and forth. She was using a phone. That could be a stroke of luck."

"It's funny, but I just can't picture any woman killing Bill. They never even got jealous because he slept around. It's too bad you didn't know him. As much as I tried, I simply couldn't find a reason to dislike him."

"Much as you tried?"

"Hell, man! Women were always coming onto *him* for bedtime sports! I work like all hell and don't get very much! I compose the perfect line to drop in at the perfect time, and they laugh in my face! He acted a little interested and they fell all over him.

"The women weren't jealous, but I was! I tried my best to get pissed about it, but it didn't work.

"What it boils down to is he was very much the type I wished I could be. I've tried to get Rita Gomez to even look at me. She doesn't know I exist.

"Rita's a real beauty who's staying across the canal. She hops right over to Bill's place anytime he snaps his fingers for her. Judy goes around with me a bit, but I know damned well he could have said one word and she'd drop me.

"The trouble is, for me to get PO'ed, he'd have to actually do something like that. I know damned well he never would."

"I've seldom come across anyone both men and women liked so consistently. Is it `Don't speak ill of the dead' or is it real?"

"I never knew anyone quite like him, either. It *is* real, at least in my case. He had a sort of balance of some kind where he was one of the guys and some kind of dream stud to the women. Bottle whatever it was and you could soon pay off the national debt with leftover pocket change."

"Well, I have to get my court order and see who called whom out there," Nick said, sighing deeply. "`Neither man nor woman would so despoil, Would ever bend or stoop, To take the nurture from this soil, E'er would kill Lord Proute.'"

"Say what?" Jamie asked, giving Nick a wary look.

"It's a quote from an English poem that seems to me more than apropos. It fits, somehow."

"Miss Amy Fletcher? I'm investigating the killing of William Rinks," Nick said, after she answered the carved mahogany door, glanced at the badge in his hand, looked him up and down and said, "Come in," in a low, husky, voice. She was tall and statuesque, with long dark hair. Bill seemed to like that type. Amy Fletcher was a knockout, and knew it.

"God, that was a shock!" she cried. "I mean, nobody would want to hurt Bill. He was just, well, like a combination guy."

"Combination guy?"

"Sort of like a close brother, on one level. You could confide in him and know it stopped right there. You could tell him anything. He'd really try to help anyone who came to him. He was also the greatest thing to happen to the American bedroom since seventeen seventy six!

"It wasn't so much that he had such a great technique, it was more that you knew he wasn't simply using you. He took time to find out about you.

"Actually, his technique was nothing to sneer at, either – Why, lieutenant! You're blushing! How refreshing!"

"Uh, you were in love with him?" Nick asked, feeling the heat in his face.

"Certainly I was in love with him! Who wasn't who ever met him? So?"

"It didn't bother you that he slept with every other woman in town?"

"He slept with a few of us he could relate to, who he could respect, and who he could love. The only drawback was that he couldn't be IN love with any of us."

"I see. Another woman used almost exactly those same words about him an hour ago. Where were you last Friday afternoon?"

"Here, mostly." She flashed a small amused smirk. "I don't have a hint of an alibi.

"Bill Rinks was far too valuable a human being for anyone to kill."

"As I replied very recently to that very same suggestion, we have to face the fact that somebody did. Can you give me any names of others he was dating regularly?"

"Bill didn't date us, lieutenant, he slept with us and cared about us.

"You're blushing again.

"Rita Gomez, Eileen Riordan, Kitty Liston, Judy Platt. I don't know how many others. Eileen and Kitty weren't around for awhile."

"I've heard of all those. Thanks."

"If that takes care of the business end, shall we see if you blush all over?" she said, grinning at him.

"Unlike the late Bill Rinks, I stick with one at the time," Nick replied, with an attempt to match the grin.

"Oh? Do I denote disapproval?" She archedg her left eyebrow.

"Strangely, no. Maybe a little jealousy."

"Well, come back to see me whenever you're in the market. I'm right here, most of the time. You don't need an appointment."

"I don't think so."

"I knew you wouldn't. I'm having some fun with you, Nick. I don't sleep around. Just with Bill, and I don't have him anymore. You're a very attractive man. I might get serious about your type, and I'm not ready for that gig, yet.

"I hope you find whoever killed Bill. I want to see them fry! Slowly. *That*, lieutenant, is not in fun!"

"Learned anything new?" Jim asked, when Nick went into the station office. "You can tell me over lunch."

Nick read the messages on his desk, put the court order in his pocket, and went with Jim and Marsha to lunch at a little Italian restaurant a few blocks away. They discussed the case, but could only decide the woman had to be either the killer or the killer's accomplice.

"She had an accomplice, that's sure!" Marsha said.

"How do you figure?" Jim asked.

"The boat stayed out there while, she didn't," Marsha replied. "She didn't walk any seven miles through mangrove swamps back."

"That's something I'll have to check, after I've finished checking the phone company," Nick agreed. "Where was the closest place she could have gone to land down there? Could the boat have drifted to where it was ... that doesn't make any sense. The boat wouldn't drift back to that close to the body. We're left with an accomplice. Period."

"It really does look that way," Jim agreed. "Like you say, she didn't walk that seven miles or more back, and nobody followed them out there. Platt and Prescott would have noticed, even if it was quite a bit later. Have you considered that?"

"Uh-huh. I think he was directed to that particular spot, somehow."

"Maybe with ship to ship rather than ship to shore?" Marsha asked. "There'd still be records."

"It still doesn't make sense, because all the larger boats carry CBs to talk back and forth on. The thing is, anyone could listen, so she'd have to use the phone if she wanted to ... suddenly I'm very curious about something!"

"What might that be?" Jim asked.

"Can I take your boat down there in the morning, Jim? I want to check on something. There is one major item that's very much out of place in what Judy Platt saw."

Jim shrugged, took out his key ring, slid off the key to his boat and flipped it to Nick. He raised an eyebrow, but didn't ask what Nick was thinking.

"I'll go out tomorrow," Nick said. "Early. I want to check with the MP for the exact location – which probably means I have to listen to Florida Marine Patrol Sergeant Samuel Robert Keller. Damn!

"I have to know the exact location of some things."

"I have his report," Marsha suggested, dryly. "Maybe the loran numbers would help? Maybe the copy of the marked charts he sent us? Maybe pages and pages of minutely detailed descriptions of the tree crabs, birds, dead fish, live fish, palm trees, shells, beer cans, seaweed and mangroves? Or maybe the angle of the sunlight through the branches over the boat? Maybe the strange kind of knot in the anchor rope?"

"I love you!" Nick cried. "The loran numbers and the charts will do.

"Strange knot in the anchor rope?"

"Yeah. Apparently a sheepshank with a fisherman's knot looped around a piece of wood, apparently builder's grade pine, two inch by two inch sawed to a length of six and one quarter inches. The one-half inch diameter bright yellow polypropylene rope was coiled under the bow on the equipment shelf that extended three quarters of the way from the point of the bow back toward...."

"Jeez! I get the idea," Jim said. "He carried a piece of wood to put in a loop to shorten the anchor rope."

"Hey, Honky! I had to write up three miserable damned pages about that stupid damned knot!" Marsha cried. "It was something standard?!"

"Sure! If you anchor in both front and back to hold you in a fishing spot you want the lines fairly tight to keep you from swinging, so you use various loop knots to shorten the rope, then pull the final loop around something. You release the whole mess by pulling out the pin or piece of wood or PVC or whatever," Jim explained. "About a third of the boats out there have something like that, if they fish the shallows."

"Crap! He thought it might have some significance, like in a satanic ritual!" Marsha cried, then started giggling. They all three got the giggles. Paddy came in to find them in a very silly mood.

"I have a court order to locate and search records of calls on ship to shore, ship to ship, or cellular, to and from this area" Nick explained to Frances Anne Parker, Supervisor and PR (And everything else. It was only a relay station) for the phone company's South Offices Station near

Everglades City. It was the closest cell and SS boost relay to the Ten Thousand Islands and Chokaloskee.

"The SS things are easy to trace, but cellular? You have to check those types of calls with the individual carriers. There are two operating down here," Frances explained. "They have towers we share on a leasing agreement with them because it would be too expensive for each company to build a tower."

"They're billed through you?" Nick asked. She just looked at him.

"This is a murder investigation." He decided to embellish, trying to get a little help. "There could be a serial killer out there. We have to trace a clue while it's fresh to save no-one-knows how many lives!"

"Oh, my dear me! What kind of serial killer? Oh, dear me!" She was almost drooling. Nick knew he had her.

"Well, this must stop right here, is that clear? We *must not* allow the killer to know we have any way to possibly track him down!"

"Oh, dear me! What's happened?"

"Well, a Naples man, Bill Rinks, went out into the gulf with a girlfriend last Friday – that's the latest victim that we know of. They found his body. He was shot. More than once. They found his boat covered with blood. Lots of violence.

"*But*! The girlfriend was *not* found! No trace of her!

"Now, there's one theory – you didn't hear this story from me. We can't stand any panic – one theory I've heard is that there's some maniac who killed Rinks and abducted the woman, possibly to hold her somewhere and repeatedly rape her, then to also kill her when he's had ... what he wants!

"It sounds like some cheap tabloid story I know, but that theory was expressed to me directly!"

"Oh, dear! I read about Mr. Rinks in the paper! It was out by the islands! My husband and I go out there all the time for blue crabs! Oh, dear! It's all so terribly *frightening*!

"I can access the computer billing records. Would that help?"

"Certainly! Mrs. Parker, you might possibly save who knows how many innocent peoples' lives with your prompt cooperation!" Nick blubbered back, as she steered him into a small office that had a computer terminal and dot matrix printer, along with a few file cabinets.

An hour later he had a list of names, times and billing numbers. He thanked Mrs. Parker and again swore her to total silence.

He took the lists back to the office, locked them in his desk, took the charts Marsha gave him out to Prescott's, then to the Banks (Who were just getting home from the boat show) to have the exact locations of everything marked, went to supper, then reported for his night shift duty.

Paddy had put Ed Goins on homicide detail night shift until further notice, so Nick poured over the lists for three hours. Nothing.

He listed everything suspicious and put the lists back into his desk. If he thought of anything else he'd want them where he could reach them quickly.

He went home to bed. In the morning he was going for a boat ride.

There were some banks of offshore fog early that quickly burned off to leave a brilliant day with a light easterly wind. The tide was high, so Nick could stay out enough to make good time. He went to the loran position where the Rinks boat was found and sighted back. He saw several long islands and hundreds of smaller odd-shaped ones peppered across the field of view.

He went slowly back northward and out into the gulf to sit about where Judy had marked they'd been on the chart. The tiny island with a thin beach of ground oyster shell on the gulfward side was easy to find from there. He went in to draw the boat onto the little fan-shaped spit and look around, picking up some beer and soda cans and some paper cartons to throw into Jim's garbage sack. What he was looking for was on the northern end of that long island nearby.

He idled the boat along and around, finding there was no wash channel there at all. It was grass flats and only five feet deep at almost high tide. As he had suspected. No one was scuba diving there at half tide on Friday. Someone put that boat at that spot, anchored it securely, and put the "diver down" flags around to keep anyone from approaching closely. The killer didn't need an accomplice. She had a boat waiting right there all the time to take in to shore.

He didn't really need to prove that, only to be able to show it as likely, but his luck was holding, so he'd see if he could find anyone who'd seen the boat being placed or who had seen it earlier.

Nick used his binoculars to view the nearby area. There were several smaller boats out in the flats, but they wouldn't be too likely to have been around Friday. He saw another little beach eastward on a small island, so went over to inspect it on the theory the killer could probably lure Rinks to a particular spot easily, then the killer could almost walk across the grass flats to the diver down boat at low tide.

There wasn't much to be found, but people had definitely been on the little sandy mound. He looked around carefully and went to get back in the boat when a little golden flash caught his eye. He bent over to carefully pick up the casing to a .25 automatic shell. He spent more than an hour minutely searching, but he couldn't find another.

A commercial fisherman went by as he was pushing the boat off and he waved, but was ignored. Jim's boat was a hell of a lot faster than the net boat, so he ran it down and held up his badge. The mullet fisherman stopped.

"I only need some information," he explained, yelling over the motor noise. "I'm out here to investigate the murder last Friday.

"There was an aluminum boat anchored out by that shell island (pointing) on the northern end with divers' flags set around. Did you see it?"

The fellow stared blankly at him a few seconds, shook his head and said, "Ain't no water there. Warn't no diver."

"I know it," Nick replied, patiently. "The killer left the boat there to take in. I want to know if you saw it."

"I ain't fishin' Friday. Didn't see nothin' at all."

"Who has the white lift front? Net boat."

"That stupid-ass thing looks like it wants to take off? Try John Putts. He's from Michigan. Don't know how to fish and ain't got sense to learn."

"Know where I can find him?"

"Back mouth of Sairy Creek north, prolly."

"Much obliged," Nick said, as he put the boat into gear. The chart showed him Sarah's Creek, so he'd find it quickly enough.

The white lift front was there, a man chatting with a woman in a green net boat with a boom light. He motored in close, avoiding the cork line carefully.

"John Putts?" he called.

"Yo! What?" the man in the lift front called back.

"I'm Nick Storie. Police. I'm here investigating the murder out here last Friday. Some people saw your boat about three thirty or so and maybe saw your friend's, too.

I need some information."

"I saw the boat they found blood in grounded on the little sandbar," Putts replied. "Maybe a quarter to four. I went by them and can't say if there were two or three people there, but I think it was only two. A man and a woman. I told that patrol clown all about it."

"Oh? Not our `Just the facts, Ma'am' expert?" Nick asked, flashing his most winning grin.

He got the grin back. "Ain't he a load?"

"I don't care about the island. There was an aluminum boat, a fourteen footer, maybe, anchored out by the gulf island on the north end. It had divers' flags around."

"Yeah. There wasn't anybody around. They probably left it with the flags so nobody'd mess with it. I went by about two hunnert feet off to eastward, but only gave it a quick once-over. That's a good spot to strike, but there weren't any fish there much. I saw it there, if that's important."

"It could be. I think the killer left it there earlier and used it to make a getaway."

"I sawr some fancy woman pullin' ut in thar," the woman on the green boat said. "She were comin' out'n fourteen. Sawr it there later on."

"You saw a woman taking it out there? She was pulling it?" Nick asked, trying to control his growing excitement. "Can you describe her? Could you identify her if called on?"

"Jist some woman. Sorta tallish. Couldn't see none've 'er much. Wearin' a yeller slicker'n a big hat."

"You're certain it was a woman?"

"Ain't no man got no legs like that'n!" She grinned, showing him a surprisingly good set of teeth. "Built like a brick shithouse, 's Putts'ud likely say.

"She were pullin' thet thar Johnboat 'long'th a beat old Glaspar. White'n 'uth sorta faded red trim. Hain't got no state numbers on't."

"OK. Two other quick questions. What time was it? Where's this fourteen?"

"'Uz mebbe sevenish or seven fifteen Friday mornin'n mouth fourteen's thet creek 'bout half a mile south.Got a old post standin' out'n ut used to have the number fourteen on a old board nailed to ut. We calls ut fourteen.

"Shaller. Careful if ya takes thet rig up't! Tide's goin' out. Get stuck'n gotta wait six – eight hours afore ut gets water tuh get out'n there."

"I might have to call on you two as witnesses when I break this case, okay?"

"Pays 'er gas'n time?"

"Not much, but the state pays mileage and a few dollars a day compensation"

"Can't be no worse'n what mullet's been bringin' in! Thet fancy woman been the killer?"

"It sure looks like it," Nick said, and waved as he backed out. He wrote down the numbers of their boats, then went back to ask, "What's your name? I didn't get it. I'm Nick."

"I'm Sweet Maggie Malone, believe't er not! He's Putts."

Nick waved again and motored back toward number fourteen. Maybe things were coming around at last! If either boat was found, they could probably trace it to somebody specific.

After forty five minutes of searching Nick located a runnel mouth with an old channel marker post standing out from it a hundred or so yards. The depth finder showed holes with washbars between them to the inside of the first curve, so he trimmed the motor up and went in slowly. The mangroves came almost together about a quarter mile in, but he managed to work the boat through to find himself sitting in a kidney-shaped bay that covered about three hundred acres. There were runnels coming in on either end, but he went as close to the mangroves as he could all the way around to be sure there were no others, then went into the southernmost runnel. About six hundred yards farther along, the runnel opened into another oval bay, perhaps fifty acres in area. There was a runnel that poured into it in back, so he went up that one for nearly another quarter mile, but the brown water kept getting shallower and branching into the reeds and mangroves. If his compass was right, he wasn't getting any closer to solid ground anywhere.

He went back to the large bay and up into the other channel. It was narrow but fairly deep and the current, with the tide going out, was fairly strong, indicating a lot of water farther in.

He crossed several small bays, while staying to the deeper flowing channel. He was in about two miles when he noticed cattails and flags along the bank.

Fresh water! This was a creek! It led into higher land!

Soon there were tall cabbage palms and low willow trees spotted here and there above the mangroves and back a few yards, so he was in an area where there was access to the creek from inland. There was quite a lot of saw grass, and ahead were willows that hung down over to virtually close off the little creek.

He cut the engine to study the banks – and heard a faint horn to his left. North. He listened intently a few minutes and heard a loud motorcycle moving at a high rate of speed. It was on a highway to be moving that fast. He'd estimate it was about a mile away.

The boat moved into the dense willow overhang as he pushed it along with the oar. It might barely squeeze through – when it hit something solid.

He went to the front and looked down to see the console of a boat just under the surface.

Nick thought a minute, then dropped the grapple anchor into the submerged boat, caught it firmly and started his engine to back slowly out from the willow overhang. The boat moved along sluggishly until it was in view.

He cut the engine, untied the anchor line from Jim's boat, and poled to the shore, where he tied the anchor line to a limb. He moved Jim's boat downstream a few yards and used another line to tie it to a stunted willow, then slopped along the muddy bank to the anchor line.

It was slow work and exhausting, but he finally had the nose of the submerged boat up on the bank enough to see it was an old white Glaspar with red trim. The drain plug had been pulled, the boat set adrift, and it caught on the overhanging willows and sank.

Nick took a stout piece of rope from Jim's boat to tie the Glaspar firmly, took the anchor back, and turned on the CB to call, "Breaker Breaker one nine. Got a smokey or county mountie out there? Breaker, breaker."

"This be the one Blue Streak Demon, ten four on county mountie," came back.

"I'm Det. Lt. Nick Storie on homicide detail. All I have on this thing is CB. Can you call FMP and have them contact me?"

"Go to channel eleven," came back. "This be the one Water Rat. We monitor nine and nineteen out here."

"Ten four. Thanks," Nick replied, and switched channels. He waited a minute, then said, "Water Rat?"

"Yo! Go!".

"Are you familiar with fourteen?"

"Yo."

"I'm up near the north-end runnel about three and half miles. I can hear some traffic noises to my left, north, maybe a mile or mile and a half away. It's shallow and narrow. I have to get this rig out of here.

"I've located a sixteen foot white Glaspar with red trim. It was scuttled. I drug it aground and tied it. I have a witness who described such a craft. It was used in the Rinks murder.

"Can you get someone in here?"

"Ten four. I'll have an air boat in there in five minutes. You'd better get out of there fast, if you're not in a canoe, or you'll be stuck for hours. There's not much water between you and the gulf, now. The place you are is within a thousand yards of the saw grass flow pond at the head of Snakebite Creek.

"Get out to the lower bays, anyhow. The air boat can't pass you in there. I'll have him wait at the last bay until you go by. You're gonna have to paddle a couple of places now, so move as fast as you can."

"Ten four!" Nick said, and started easing Jim's boat down the creek. He had to push the boat across one shallow bar before the first bay. The air boat was waiting there and waved him to go on. He got on the CB and explained. They told him to get out as fast as he could – or he might not get out for more than ten hours, when the tide would be full enough to move.

He had to push the heavy boat across two more shallow spots. He was swearing on the last one because he wasn't sure he could get it across, but he managed it. He was exhausted again as he ran into the large lower bay to find the MP shallow-draft boat there. He chatted with them for a few minutes. They couldn't go any farther upstream in even that boat, but the air boat was carrying Paddy's lab crew to the Glaspar. The air boat pulled it upstream to a little ridge where a swamp buggy could get in close and Paddy was called.

Nick finally went out into the gulf, found deeper water and headed for home. He had plenty, so far, but he still

needed a few small items before it was sewed up com-
pletely. Those phone calls were the one thing that could do
it, but none of his suspects seemed to have *made* any calls
from out there.

Chapter three

"I see you've had a very busy day!" Marsha greeted, as Nick went into the office. "Paddy and Jim went with Tiny to check over that boat. Jim tells me that a Glaspar has the serial numbers stamped directly into the transom, so it doesn't matter if there aren't any state numbers.

"You got maybe a bunch of notes I can type up, huh? Do you? Huh? Pant! Pant! Huh?"

"Interested in this one?" Nick asked.

"I've read your case notes through yesterday. That lock on your desk takes ten seconds to open with a piece of wire and a penknife.

"This one reads like a soap opera! I wish I'd met that guy! I ever find Hank sleeping with any other woman I'll cut it *off* for him! None of those nutty women cared if he slept around?"

"No, I really don't think they did, in that way. They seemed to expect it of him. It doesn't make any sense to me, either, but I think they're all pretty sincere about it.

"I have four main suspects. There has to be some way to tie one of them to it."

"Four? I'd think you'd have forty!"

"Nope! I only have Amy Fletcher, Rita Gomez, June Cerf – and any other tall, dark-haired woman with a great shape who ever slept with him. That's four. You're tall and dark-haired. You ever sleep with him?"

"Me? I'm dark all over. Lorna Fields has to be on your little list. You've never spoken with Mel.

"Did you ever stop to think the hair might have been a wig?"

"Uh-huh! I even considered some guy dressed up as a woman, but nobody could have done that after the time the slacks were shed for the bathing suit. Nobody could have fooled Rinks for one minute that way, either. It wasn't Lorna, because two other people saw her on the boat with Mel."

"Not at the time the murder was committed."

"But it was *not* Lorna Jamie Prescott and Judy Platt saw out there with him."

"Okay. It was one of those three or who?"

"Al Terns' daughter, Ellen."

"What the...! You haven't even seen her and she's not even in the state!"

"I'm not all that sure of that. She's been described to me by three people as being a beauty and as having slept with Rinks. Al told me she was in Milwaukee and gave me her address and phone number. I've called her several times and get a machine. She isn't there.

"I've traced two others, Kitty and Eileen. I got to both of them within a couple of hours."

"Wouldn't Al have recognized his own daughter on that boat that close?"

"He said the woman looked familiar, somehow, but he didn't know why. She was bundled up like that maybe so HE wouldn't recognize her?"

"Well, here's the lists of what was found at his place." She handed him a file folder. "You might want to go over it yourself. The new owners won't arrive here until tomorrow, so nothing's been touched, yet. You'd know more about what to look for than the crew."

"I think I'll go over there on my way home. Give the keys to Jim, will you? Tell him I filled the tank on the county's bill. I was using it for official business.

"I will be thoroughly *damned*! Here's a spent shell casing from a twenty five automatic I found out by the island! It was that one just inside the long barrier island I marked on the chart. I forgot it until I reached in my pocket just now! It's bagged, but it won't have anything after being under salt water for so long. Maybe a pin mark Tiny can use, or his ballistics department.

"I also found a couple of witnesses about the divers' boat out there. It's all in the notes. They know they could be called to testify.

"I'll spend tomorrow morning trying to find which of those calls are of any significance. I'm much too tired to worry about it now."

"The diver's boat? The witnesses? The casing from the murder shot?" Marsh said, wide-eyed. "What the Sam hell else has slipped whatever passes for your mind?"

He grinned and went out.

There was probably nothing in Rinks' house that would help with the case. Nick didn't think so from the first, or he'd have gone to the house while he was out there, anyhow, before the crew got there to move everything around.

He went through it very carefully, looking over the papers he found in a drawer in the kitchen and pocketing the book of addresses and phone numbers next to the phone. He found a stack of letters in a desk drawer in a remodeled bedroom. The room was furnished with a long writing/ computer desk along one side and contained a lot of electronic musical instrumentation and several sets of drums.

He shoved the letters into a paper bag to take along to read later, then checked the computer disks, but they seemed to be some kind of music programs he didn't begin to understand.

Rinks had been a hell of a lot neater than most bachelors, but still not too extreme. The place was clean, but it was disordered. He couldn't tell if anyone had been searching there before him – like maybe the murderer – looking for some incriminating clue.

He finally sighed heavily, shook his foggy head and headed for home. He was in that state of physical exhaustion that makes sleep impossible, so he turned on the TV for awhile and tried to forget the case. After about two hours he went to bed and was able to finally drop off.

"The old boat was last registered to a Marvin Randall Shackleford in Starke, Florida," Paddy reported the next morning, when Nick and Jim went into his office for a briefing. "Shackleford gave it to some kids to fix up. They patched the small crack in the bottom and sold it to `some old guy in a rusty old brown Ford pickup for twenty bucks.

"That's all we have. The kids sanded the FL numbers off and repainted it. That was done eight years ago. The boat was launched a couple hundred feet from the Trail across the saw grass. There's a rough limestone road a little way into the swamp there that canoe fishermen use. We could trace where the boat crushed the grass in spots.

"The aluminum job would be easier to get in and out than the Glaspar. Nobody saw anything, for certain, but some kids who live a couple miles farther out said there was an old car parked there all day Friday."

"How did she get the car there?" Nick asked.

"The Trailways bus stops at a filling station one and three quarter miles back this way," Paddy said. "We checked with all the drivers. There's always someone in charge there, and they picked up several women, but none who would fit our descriptions. One driver said he saw a woman walking toward Naples at about nine ten carrying a yellow gas can, but she waved him on when he slowed. He said all he remembered about her was that she was wearing a yellow rain slicker and fishing boots – and a big straw hat."

"Very clever!" Nick said. "That was her. She leaves the old car there and takes a ride with the first out of state tourist heading north. No witness!"

"You're fairly sure?" Jim asked.

"The fisherman – or fisher*woman* – saw her pulling the aluminum boat out. She was wearing a big straw hat and a rain slicker, but no boots."

"What kind of old car?" Marsha asked. "The one the kids saw parked there Friday morning."

"It was rust brown and one of those square things from the early seventies or late sixties," Paddy answered. "They say they didn't get close. I suppose they don't steal things out of old wrecks like that."

"Paddy! How cynical!" Jim laughed. "True, but cynical.

"What do we look for?"

"Why would she know about that place at all?" Nick asked. "None of my suspects is the type to run around swamps to ever know about such a place in case she ever needed it, and how in hell would she know the creek leads into the gulf?

"Damn it! I *know* this case is laid out and crystal clear! I just can't read it! I'm missing something obvious!"

"Maybe the one you haven't met yet is the outdoorsy type," Marsha suggested. "I tried calling the number, and only got an answering machine."

"Well, if we get a call back sometime this afternoon I'll really get suspicious of her," Nick said, grimly. "That would be timing with a little too much coincidence thrown in. The problem with that is it would throw my main suspect out of the whole thing.

"Well, maybe not that much. I have some other things to check out. Maybe the answer'll turn up in this crap. I have the tedious part to go through now. I hate the working from a list part.

"I'll have to solve this one before Saturday. I have a date."

"Say! Maybe Janet knew Rinks! She's tall, has a great shape and has long dark hair!" Marsha said, leering evilly.

"Hey, now, you! There are *some* things we don't joke about!" Nick retorted. "Say! Marsha, get me the missing vehicle report for the past two weeks."

Ed Goins came in and Paddy said he'd remain in charge of the night shift for another day or two. Jim, Marsha and Nick went back to their respective desks. Paddy went into his office with Ed.

Nick dropped the sack of letters from Rinks' house on his desk and dropped the phone/address book in the drawer, poured a cup of coffee, and sat to look through them.

He hated reading other people's mail. These were mostly from women who were asking for his advice of a nature he found too embarrassingly personal in nature. Kitty, Eileen and Ellen wrote to Rinks sporadically. There wasn't very much in the letters that could damage them when you considered that everyone knew they'd slept with him. The letters weren't very erotic. They either asked for his advice or thanked him for advice already given.

He put one aside from someone who merely signed the letter with "Corrie". She told about a skiing trip to Colorado, then: *I know what you meant in your last letter about your problem. I hope you can make her understand your feelings about that kind of situation. She is not reacting rationally, because you would never do anything to hurt her with him.*

Bill, she has to understand your position. No one who knows you would believe you would ever do those things. She is acting like a true paranoid type of person. Are you

I don't know her very well, but if she doesn't come to her senses soon I will try to talk to her...

There was no date and no envelope and there was no name except "Corrie".

So everything was not quite so perfect with everybody in this! Some woman was "acting like a true paranoid" where Rinks was concerned!

Apparently a boyfriend (Or husband? Maybe she'd told him she wasn't married?) was onto him and was causing her trouble of some sort.

Ellen always ended her letters with a suggestion he come to live with her, but so did several others.

This was the first lead not connected to the case by the events surrounding the actual killing. It could be important, or it could be another big fat zero.

Nick sighed and read the rest of the letters, then opened the file Marsha left on his desk. Rinks' bank statements were normal, except for one item. A couple of hundred dollars a month to some woman in Louisiana.

He kept all his canceled checks and the deposit receipts in a box in the desk drawer. He was most definitely not being blackmailed, nor had he been receiving any blackmail-type payments. He made a lot of money (compared to a cop's salary) and he gave a lot of it away, but nothing to any pattern. No sudden large sums going either direction, no mysterious checks on the third Friday of every month for an even five thousand dollars.

Nothing.

His IRS forms were exact to the last penny. He was, apparently, a rare truly honest type. There was a sheet in the back of the bank statements file explaining that the two hundred dollars a month was for child support. Rinks was helping to pay for the raising of a biracial young boy.

There were no records of the child's birth.

Maybe Rinks had fathered a child who would inherit. That point would have to be checked. He called over to Marsha to ask her to start the wheels turning on that.

Nick sighed again and sat back, then picked up the address book to try to locate Corrie, but found nothing.

There was one page missing from the book! A Dorine Carlson was followed by a Laurie Dodd! There was a little fuzz down between the pages where it had been torn out, carefully. That could merely be a coincidence. It could be a deliberate attempt to divert suspicion onto the one suspect who was in that part of the alphabet, June Cerf – after all, it would be perfectly natural for him to have both her numbers. He worked at the restaurant with the band. Nothing else in the book caught his attention. There wasn't anything for it now but to start trying to find something in that SS and cellular phone list.

He dreaded that! A vitally important answer was definitely somewhere in that, but what? None of those calls originated from a phone registered to *any* of the suspects.

He also had to connect how the killer knew about the place where she launched the boats. That a woman could do it, he didn't doubt. A trailer with a winch and that light aluminum boat. She could have dropped the motor from the old Glaspar into the aluminum job, then cranked the whole thing up. The only hard part would be getting the Glaspar across the grass in the first place, but there had been enough rain to have made the little saw grass lake a couple of inches deeper on Thursday. That's all it would take. The creek would drop the water level in a few hours.

He called the airport weather station for the record. There had been one and a half inches of rain, with only a light southwesterly wind south of Naples along the coast Thursday morning. That was another little item for his chart.

Marsha came over to hand him a computer readout of the vehicles reported stolen recently. She'd painted a yellow highlighter on one item: "1968 Chrysler Imperial, Brown, four door. Stolen from U Partem Auto Salvage, Immokalee, Thursday, May 7, 1992. Vehicle was outside the wall and was in good running condition. Needed only a battery. Stolen between 8:00 PM and 11:00 PM. VIN # ...."

"You think maybe that was our square old brown car?" Nick asked.

"Read all about it on the next page, Sherlock," Marsha suggested, grinning.

The highlight there: "1968 Chrysler Imperial, VIN # ... found abandoned in wooded area of Golden Gate May 13, 1992, traced to the...."

"Paddy went to check it a few minutes ago," she said. "Want to bet?"

"Nope! Not even maybe! We're closing in on this one, Marsh. If I can find a couple more things, we've got our killer."

"Well, it's past my lunch time. Take me out and I'll help with those numbers."

"You're on!" Nick agreed.

"Hi! Here's Tiny's forensic report on the car," Marsha said upon returning to her desk from lunch. "Want to see it?"

Nick took the pages and glanced at them. He noted the more important things, such as the fact the car had a trailer hitch with a small utility trailer ball in it.

For pulling a boat trailer?

The ball was scarred from recent use. There were no fingerprints in the car other than those of the regular people working at the junkyard. The last driver apparently wore soft (cotton?) gloves that smudged over everything on the steering wheel, the gearshift buttons and anything else touched.

Nick flipped on through the report, then asked Marsha to buzz Tiny on the interphone.

He came on.

"Tiny? Have you printed the battery box and hood latch on that old Chrysler?"

"The hood latch. We didn't print the battery itself, no. Why?"

"When that car was stolen, it didn't have a battery. It had a battery when you checked it?"

"Hang on!" Tiny cried, and Nick could hear him yelling for somebody to get back to that car and to very carefully remove the battery without touching it and bring it in to the lab. Yesterday!

"It's an older used battery," Tiny finally said. "We can hope. I didn't have anything to make me think of it. Thanks for the tip. Probably saved my ass."

"There are several cars in running order in the front of that yard," Marsha said. "I called them. They sell the ones they have clear titles for to collectors. They leave out the batteries and put the keys over the visor."

"So we've got a very concise picture of everything – except for who pulled the trigger," Nick mused. "I keep getting the feeling it's all there staring us in the face. I haven't put all the figures into the right columns yet."

He went to sit at his desk to enter the pieces about the car into his notes in their proper spots. He always made a sort of chart of boxes he could fill in. The order of squares took him moment by moment through the crime, the entry was made when the evidence was tight.

His phone buzzed and he reached for it, glancing up to

see Marsha staring oddly at him.

"Storie," he said.

"Lt. Storie? This is Ellen Terns. I have several messages on my machine to please call you?"

He was almost dumbfounded, but made a fast recovery. "I've been trying to reach you for several days. I have some bad news, if you haven't heard, and I need to ask you a question or two."

"Bad news? Is Dad all right?!"

"He's fine. This is about Bill Rinks."

"Bill? I don't understand."

"I'm afraid I have the extremely unpleasant duty to inform you he's dead. He was murdered," Nick said, not quite knowing which direction to take this. He waited into the stunned silence for a few moments more, then, "Miss Terns?"

"Oh, dear God in heaven! Tell me this is some kind of insane sick joke!"

"I'm afraid not. I'm sorry. I learned from your father that you dated Mr. Rinks and must know if you are aware of *any* fact, any smallest fact whatever, that could help us in finding a direction to take in this kind of investigation. It seems Mr. Rinks was liked by everyone he met."

"I have to call Dad! I know he's been trying to call, but he won't leave a message on the machine. He just hangs up if I don't.... Oh, God!

"Not Bill! Please! Not Bill!"

"Miss Terns, if you know of anything, no matter how small, we *must* know!"

"I don't believe you! No one would hurt Bill!"

"I'll get control of myself in just a minute. I have to! Just give me a minute to think."

"Where have you been for the past few days? You should leave an emergency number with someone. A message about how to contact you. Can't you call your phone and get your messages?"

"I was in New York for a shoot. This won't sink in. It won't.

"What happened? When?"

"A shoot?"

"I'm modeling for Crest Cosmetic Arts International. Would it be better if I called Dad?"

"He's probably very worried he can't reach you. Maybe if you could tell me when...."

She hung up!

Nick looked at Marsha, who had been listening to the whole conversation on her extension. She shrugged and said, "I'll call the agency, but she was there or she wouldn't have dared to say she was. SHE ain't it!"

Nick sighed for the ten thousandth time for the day and sat back to think. Anything to keep from doing what he knew he'd have to do, now. Those lists of phone numbers were the tedium that often made this kind of work less than pleasant.

Another sigh, then he picked up the list. It was times and caller ID codes with the destination numbers on the first of several sheets, then a sheet of the numbers and who they were registered to on another. That second one was easily the biggest disappointment, so far, because none of the numbers was registered to anyone he knew to be involved in the case.

"Marsh?" he called. "Can you get me cellular numbers for all the businesses ... wait. I have a listing in here somewhere ... here it is. Hmmm. J. Prescott has a cellular car phone.... Cerf's Surf has a cellular *and* car phone.... Mel Sharpe has a cellular car phone. Rita Gomez has one and Amy Fletcher has one.

"Why in *Hell* would every damned suspect in this stupid

mess have one of the miserable damned things?!"

"Because they're all in the higher brackets and a cellular phone's a status symbol," Marsha replied, putting a cup of black coffee on his desk and pulling up a chair. "I think they ought to outlaw the things! Have you seen the way some people drive while they're chatting away?

"As for that point, what do you think of that stupid ad on TV?"

"Marsh, what in the hell are you talking about?"

"That cell phone ad. Some idiot's wife is having a baby, she's in the car, moaning – and he's calling the hospital on his handy-dandy cell phone – while backing out of his driveway onto a busy street! The phone's in one hand, a pregnant woman moaning on the seat next to him, driving a car backward out into a busy street with one hand while looking over the back of the seat!

"What do you think of the ads telling how powerful Rising Sun Motors' new Super Turbocharged V-six can pass a big tanker truck in a flash – going up a blind hill on a blind curve?

"Crazy, man! What a thrill! Did you ever notice the ad about most sinus medicines making you drowsy, but Brand X doesn't? Then why is it that the doofus who took the crud being advertised was driving on the wrong side of the road when she had to swerve to miss the one who took the sleep-inducing garbage – who was driving normally?

"The morons who come up with those ads are on crack, right?"

"You sure are wound up. Here. Look for any of these numbers on those sheets and I'll check these." He handed her half the printouts.

Forty minutes later they had nothing. Zilch. None of their numbers were called or made calls in the area.

"Well? Now what?" Marsha asked.

"Damn it all, Marsh! We *know* she made several calls out there! We *know* ... wait a minute! We know she made one at about three o'clock from the end of the channel into Royal Rubbish Acres. I have to get the numbers from right there at that time, then we match them to this list and we have a very good start.

"I'm on my way to the phone company. My court order will cover it."

"There's another possibility," Marsha cautioned. Nick raised his eyebrows at her.

"Did it ever occur to you she may not have actually made any calls?"

"Uh-huh. I don't want to think about that. She might have made it a point to be seen talking on a cell phone out there by several people so we'd try to trace the calls and come up with nothing or the wrong suspect. If we tried to base a case on phone calls, we'd have to produce records of those calls, or the case would collapse. That's why I've put the calls to the side, so to speak. I'm building the case from several angles. If the phone thing falls through it's not going to hurt us, I promise!"

Marsha gave him the victory "V" sign and a tight grin, then started pushing the sheets back into the file.

Nick left.

"What I have to find is what calls were made from this area, area S twelve on your map, between a quarter to three and three thirty PM on Friday afternoon," Nick explained to the arrogant jerk, "Mr. Elton Hobbs – Flr. Sup." according to the little name tag on his pocket, at the phone company's main billing offices. "This is a capital murder investigation. This is a court order."

"Serve it on the cellular carriers, then!" the jackass Nick was talking to snapped.

"I'm serving it on you," Nick said, silkily. "If you fail to comply with this order your tail cools a cell for contempt of court, capich?"

"Ship to shore and marine cellular calls do *not* go through this office!"

"The billing does, and that's the fastest way to get what we need."

"Tough shit! Some hotshot *flatfoot* doesn't scare *me*!" the ass retorted. "You might want to try to prove *that* one to a judge! I'm busy!"

Nick yanked the cuffs from his belt and slapped one side on his wrist and the other to the jerk.

"You are under arrest on the charge of contempt of lawfully executed court order A five seven four four dash six six seven nine. You have the right to remain silent. Should you choose to give up that right...."

"Hey! Hey! What the hell do you think you're doing?!" Hobbs yelled.

Other people were coming to stare in the door. One woman winked and gave Nick a "Thumbs up." Apparently Flr. Sup. Mr. Elton Hobbs wasn't too popular with his underlings.

"I'm arresting you for contempt of court. Now you go downtown for the booking, fingerprinting and mug shots, then you go before Judge Collins to explain why you defied her order in a capital murder case.

"Let's see ... if you give up that right anything you say can and will be used against you in a court of law. You have the right of an attorney's presence during any questioning. If you cannot afford one the court will appoint one.

"Do you understand these rights?

"Okay then! Let's go! I think you'll *really* enjoy the strip and body cavity searches!"

"But I don't *have* the stuff you want here! This is crazy! That stuff isn't even *here*!"

"That's funny. It was a matter of only a few seconds down in the Everglades City branch. You see, I'm going to produce the readouts from down there for the judge, which will prove beyond any reasonable doubt that you *do* have the stuff here, and that all you're doing is pulling an act to impress these people – which I'm sure you did, but not the way you planned. I think ninety days in a cell ought to give you plenty of time to think it over, don't you?

"Let's go!"

"I'm not going anywhere!"

"Oh, good! You're resisting arrest! Want to take a swing at me? That makes it a felony. Resist with violence, you know."

"What is going on in here?" a woman asked, coming in through the crowd at the door.

"Mrs. Stewart! This damned *flatfoot* is trying to arrest me!" Elton whined.

"Trying to? Oh, come *on*! I just *did*!" Nick pointed out.

"What's going on here, officer?" she asked.

Nick handed her the court order, and said, "Mr. Hobbs refuses to comply. I'm taking him in for booking."

"What do you need from us here, officer?"

Nick repeated what he needed.

"Angela! Get me a printout from cell billing. Area S twelve from fourteen forty five to sixteen hundred thirty on the eighth of this month. SS and C one and two," she said to a girl near the door. "Officer, if you would release Mr. Hobbs in my custody, I will fully assure you this kind of thing will never happen again. Our policy is to always cooperate with law enforcement agencies. Mr. Hobbs has embarrassed the company. He will not have a second chance to do that."

"You stupid goddamned dyke bitch!" Hobbs screamed. "You think you're so hot! Big bad boss over us men! You've been waiting to get me! You know damned well you stole my promotion! You've always been out to get me!"

"To tell the truth, I have," she agreed quietly. "You are and always were unqualified for your position.

"Officer?"

Nick grinned at her and unlocked the handcuffs. Angela returned with several pages of printout. Nick thanked Mrs. Stewart and left. Elton was fuming and cursing everyone in the company who let "a bunch of bull dykes take a man's job!" This case was weird, but he was getting used to it. A cop came across all types. Elton Hobbs was going to be looking for a job in a saturated labor market – and he was *not* going to find one in management.

"I'll compare these cellphone numbers," Marsha suggested. "If any of them match, we can use it. If not, we know it was a ruse.

"Paddy and Tiny are in the gloom room right now. Jim's in, and Ed."

Nick nodded, and went on into Paddy's office. "Anything I need to know?"

"No. No prints on the battery," Tiny replied. "It's been wiped. It's a little lawnmower battery, anyhow."

"Lawnmower battery? Would that start that big car?"

"Yo. They have gear-driven starters on Chrysler products, It would eat the battery up after awhile, but it would work a few times.

"There was some gasoline with two-cycle oil spilled on the rear floorboard between the rear and front seats, so the gas can was carried there. The Glaspar had green algae growing below the natural water line, so it had been in the water for at least a week before Friday."

"Crap. I'd hoped it was launched on Thursday when the extra rainwater filled the saw grass pond."

"It was. The algae was scraped from going across the grass. It was moved from somewhere else."

"I don't think so," Jim argued. "I think it was left up at that end of the pond, which means the murder was planned at least a week before."

"I'll have to go back out there and look around," Nick said. "I'll need a map to get me to the exact spot. I also need the names of those kids. The ones who saw the car on Friday."

"You do?" Paddy asked.

"Did you ask them if they'd seen the Glaspar somewhere else around that pond?"

Jim grinned. Paddy shook his head.

"You stated you very much wanted to know how the killer even knew about that place," Ed said. "I didn't have much to do last night and had to go through some county records, so I had them print out the tax records for the whole area. Maybe you'll recognize a name on it. I put the printout on your desk."

"Thanks, Ed. That'll save me a lot of time."

There wasn't anything else for Nick, so he went to his desk to look over the tax records. He didn't recognize anything there, but put the lists with the rest of his paperwork.

Marsha handed him a listing with nine numbers that had called from both areas in the gulf within the time-frames. He didn't see anything, so said he was going hunting in the reed swamps. Marsha shook her head and grinned.

"You've had a complaint filed against you. Some guy named Hobbs claims that you beat him up and threatened him with arrest without cause.

"I told him Internal Affairs' number and said to make

certain he had backup witnesses because you could charge him with making a false complaint if he was shown to be acting in spite."

"I don't need any IA investigation right now!" Nick snapped.

"I assured him you would never file those charges against him without being able to prove due cause, so he could go ahead and file his complaint." She grinned.

"Okay! What DID you tell him I'd do?"

"Oh, I said you always had the option of suing the piss out of him for a false claim that indicated, as his complaint implied, that you had made any physical assault on him without provocation. I then explained what provocation is. I don't think you'll be hearing anything more out of your *dear* friend, Hobbs!"

"What is provocation?".

"In this case?" she answered, with a giggle. "Anything like resisting a lawful court order would place him under criminal contempt, which would mean you could arrest him with whatever force you deemed necessary. If he resisted arrest in any violent way you could go so far as to blow his stupid head off for him!

"I explained that resisting arrest was filed either without violence or with violence. If it was without violence he could only get a few months in the pen. If he took a swing at you you were free to do anything you wanted. I also told him if you had given him his rights, he was under arrest, and that he remained under that arrest until you officially released him. Personally. No one else could do that.

"He said you released him in Mrs. Stewart's custody, so I said, so long as you directly stated you were releasing him from arrest, he was out of that part of it, but if you merely allowed Mrs. Stewart to take over without formally stating that he was released he was still under arrest, legally."

"So what?"

"Why, I explained that you could come pick him up anytime in the next two years for any reason whatever, such as if you were in a lousy mood or maybe just PO'ed about phone solicitors calling every night when you were trying to fix your supper, or getting in the shower, or something. The charges he was arrested on remain active for *two whole years!*

"He's a total nutcase. I'm glad he didn't know I'm black. It was bad enough that a stupid bull dyke was handling a man's job there."

"He seems to have a problem about a female boss. He was trying to show the staff there how to handle a common flatfoot. It backfired, and he doesn't have the brains to drop it. The whole world's conspiring to make him look like the fool he is. There's going to be some other kind of trouble from that one. Count on it!

"I'm going out to the pond. I'll stop in before the end of the day. I have a little idea to try out.

"I keep saying we have to cover all the angles and we've been looking at the phone calls from the wrong one.

"Later!" He went out to his car.

Nick had to walk in from just a few yards from the Tamiami Trail. His car wasn't designed to go into that kind of morass. He could see where swamp buggies had come through, and even found one spot where the Chrysler had driven out. The big heavy car wouldn't stick with the solid lime rock undersurface only a few inches below, and the suspension would handle the pounding. If the boat hadn't been tied down tight it would get beat up on the light trailer, but she probably went out dead slow through the bad parts.

The shallow saw grass pond stretched out for several acres. It had a webbing of narrow ditch-like channels running through it, making Nick wonder how she got to that boat if it was left out there anywhere.

The bus driver said she was wearing fisherman's boots. Hip boots!

The bottom had an inch or two of light sticky mud. It was basically lime rock under that, so she probably simply waded to wherever the boat was kept.

He sighed and dropped anything the water might damage into an evidence bag and sealed it, shoved it into his shirt pocket, and slipped into the muddy water, taking a six foot piece of thin branch from the edge of the path to feel for the depth ahead of him. Mostly, it was less than eighteen inches.

After about another hour and a half of slogging among the shallow channels while fighting through the razor-like saw grass he found an old willow stump with wear marks from a rope around it. The Glaspar could have been tied there and wouldn't be visible from the pathway where people could come in. There was still a slight shallow triangular groove into the bank right up to the stump. He'd have trouble getting back to that exact spot unless he could mark it.

Nick was resourceful. He attached his white hand-kerchief to the stick he was carrying and stood it alongside the stump base. He pushed it in as far as it would go, but it still tended to fall over. There was rock less than a foot under the surface of the soggy soil.

The saw grass was as tough as rope. He used his pen-knife to cut and weave a cord and tied the stick to the stump. It was solid.

He went back out to the path. When he looked back he could see the white of the handkerchief about ten inches above the saw grass.

There wasn't anything else to see, so he sloshed back to his car, got an old rubberized tarp out of the trunk to cover the seat, and climbed in to radio for Tiny to send someone out with a canoe to take a cast of the indentation in the bank and some pictures of the stump.

"Why do we need the print cast?" Tiny asked.

"Because it's going to fit the nose of that Glaspar pulled out of the creek. Exactly. It's another small detail, but you know how I am. If there's ever any question I want to be able to prove *that* boat was tied to *that* stump."

"You do worry about those details. You'll have your cast."

Another little box filled in on his chart.

Nick backed out and rechecked the addresses Paddy gave him. He drove back to where he found three preteenage boys working on a log playhouse on the higher bank of the canal near where one of the kids on Paddy's list lived, so he called, "Juan? Juan Oliviez?"

All three came to stare at him.

"You should take off your pants when you go swimming, man!" one of them said. "I'm Juan. What you want?"

"I'm a cop. Nick.

"I need to know if any of you saw the old fiberglass boat they pulled out of the creek before?"

"Old man Pickleface put it there," one of them said. "He put it there every year. He tied it to a pipe or somethin'."

"Old man Pickleface?"

"Yeah. We call him Ol' Pickleface," Juan said. "He's really dumb, man! That cruddy boat's too big for in there!"

"Yeah! He told us if anybody touched his boat he'd have us in jail," another said. "Stupido! Like he could have us put in jail just because somebody touched his stupid boat? Right, man!"

"You don't know his name, I guess?"

"He's always Ol' Pickleface," Juan replied. "Real old! Stingy cheap bastard. Anybody else'd give us a buck or two to see nobody fucked with his boat."

"What kind of car did he drive?"

"Old rusty Ford truck that looks like it won't make it to town and back," Juan said. "Cheap old bastard got money up his ass and won't even buy a good car."

"He use the boat for fishing?"

They looked at each other, shrugged, and said they'd never seen him take any fishing equipment out with him. He didn't live anywhere around there.

Curiouser and curiouser. Nick made a few notes and sat to consider for a minute before driving slowly back toward the station for Marsha to fuss over his being wet and cold.

"Cold?! It's eighty eight degrees out there! I wasn't cold until I came in here where you keep it at forty five degrees!

"Marsha? Why was that damned boat out there, and what did Old Pickleface use it for? More importantly, how did our killer know about it?"

"What, besides fishing, is there to do in a boat out there? Run drugs?" she returned.

"That far in? In those conditions? When he couldn't get in or out more than two thirds of the time?"

"Maybe there's a pot patch in there? The kids did say he put it there every year."

"Damn! Now I have to do anoth ... no I don't! That isn't my case! No way! Call the DEA and make a suggestion they check anywhere he could go in that boat from in there. I have to worry about a murder, not pot.

"Still, how did our murderer know about the boat at all? None of my suspects are, as so aptly noted, the outdoorsy types who would ever go 'way out there to plod around in a dirty swamp for any reason I can picture.."

"She might have gone out there with somebody else for some reason or other. Maybe her boyfriend hunts frogs out there. I heard some of them do that."

"But there isn't anything out there! Nothing but miles and miles of swamp! Frogs, you can get in the ditches by the road. Why go to that much trouble?"

"Then she went out there specifically to see a swamp. It's what you have. Eliminate the impossible and go with what's left. That's all that's left.

"So why would anyone want to see a swamp?"

"Maybe somebody sold a.... Maybe.... I've got this lovely swamp to sell you, cheap! It's not *always* a joke – especially to anyone who's *bought* one of those famous Florida swamps! Ed even supplied me with nice tax plots."

"Except Rinks didn't sell anybody any Florida swamp or anything else." Marsha reminded.

"Ah! Maybe he knew who *did*! Maybe a little bit of motive's finally coming through this thing!"

He sat and took out the tax rolls to pour over them. He had to get a plot map sent over so he'd know where each holding was.

It was all held by various companies, what little wasn't state land. That meant another round of tedium, pouring over the charters.

"The angle! I almost forgot about that point!" he suddenly cried. "Marsh, hand me those phone lists. Something just rang a bell. A phone bell!"

"There's one other little juicy item you may want to hear about," Marsha said. "Your friend Elton Hobbs?

"Mrs. Stewart charged him with felony assault and battery and will prosecute, as she puts it, `Until Satan passes by my back door on snowshoes!'

"It seems she was explaining to the personnel manager

about his behavior. He called her a few choice and very unflattering epithets, then took a swing at her. She crowned him with the marble pen set from the manager's desk. Concussion city! He's under a fifteen grand bond."

"Well! *Some*thing went right today!" Nick said brightly.

Chapter four

Nick was seated at his desk, comparing the various lists, while Marsha watched him with a concerned expression. She knew how he could have a set of facts hidden somewhere in his mind, and those facts would suddenly line up in such a way to make a case suddenly clear. That "phone bell" remark made her certain he'd done it again, but she could also see there was something missing. He was also going to get a surprise when he read the report from Louisiana.

He took out a sheet of paper to start listing events in chronological order. The switchboard lit up and Marsha went to work. Ed Goins came in and went directly to Nick with a couple of report forms. Nick looked up. "What you got, Ed?"

"I figured you'd want to trace the aluminum boat and had a little time. It's slow this time of year.

"I found it."

"I could kiss you!"

"I don't think my wife would approve, and I know quite surely I wouldn't," Ed said, seriously. Nick never quite knew when Ed was joking, but caught the little sparkle in his eye, and grinned. He took the reports.

"I sorted through the reports of all missing boats. It seems your murderer likes to steal things, so it seemed a logical step."

The first sheet was a missing vehicle report. It stated that a fourteen foot aluminum bass boat on a trailer had been stolen from Gadson's Fish Camp, who was a dealer in that brand of boat, along with a ten horsepower motor from another boat from in front of the camp between the hours of 1:00 AM and 2:30 AM Friday, May 8. The padlocks

Page 79

were cut off of the retainer chains, then the thief simply drove off with the boat. There was a lot of other information included, but that was basically it.

The second sheet was a merchandise recovery report that stated the boat and extra motor were found parked to the side of the camp on opening Saturday morning. No one knew when it was put back there, but it was after midnight Friday, when the camp was closed. A standard printing and evidence search was conducted, but no prints etc....

It was a total dead end. All they knew was the boat disappeared one night and was back the next. The working assumption was that someone unknown wanted to go fishing and didn't want to rent or buy a boat. The motor had been run in salt water.

"Thanks, Ed," Nick said. "This fills in a few gaps nicely. I have this case solved I think, but these little details tie things together in a noose around a killer's neck. Each new added detail's another loop!"

"If I may suggest, don't try to be poetic, Sir. You really aren't," Ed said, but this time he couldn't quite stop the flash of a grin.

Ed went into Paddy's office while Nick entered the times and dates on his chronological chart, then sat to think a moment.

The next step was the tax rolls. He found the parts he needed, then swung his computer monitor around and started asking the machine questions. He wasn't very good at it, so called Marsha over.

"Marsh, I need to find the ownership of corporations. I can find most of it, but not what I need."

"Give me an example."

"Clearblue Realty Brokers, Inc. They're on Paradise and Meadow Lark off Davis. Four seventeen."

She called up realty, which showed nine type listings on

the screen. She touched the box marked "Reg. Brokers" with the stylus, which brought up nine more boxes.

She asked what kind of brokers they were.

"I've no vaguest idea. Just listed as brokers on the tax rolls."

"Well? It's time to let your fingers do the walking!" She grinned, so he grabbed the phone book, flipped through to the yellow pages, and read out, "Wholesale, retail, large tracts, estate holdings and related investments."

She touched the stylus to "General" and a long list came on the screen. She scrolled down to "Clearblue Realty," which had four companies. She touched "Large tracts Dev."

"Clearblue Realty Holdings <Overview Land Trust Investors, Inc. <Hodgkinson Diversified."

She then touched the stylus to "Hodgkinson Diversified" and said, "So! It was the Cerf bitch. How you gonna prove it?"

Mr. Arnold Thomas Hodgkinson, sole prop./C.E.O. was on the screen.

"With a phone call. I have this one figured out, now. It's early enough no one will be there. I'll have to find a solid connection with only one number. I already have it with the other.

"Have Paddy and whoever else wants in on this one in Paddy's office in about ten minutes? Ed should be in on it."

He picked up the data sheet received from Louisiana, read it a moment and cried, "And *there's* my motive! Bigger than *Hell*, there's my *motive*!"

"Here's what I have right now, and what I think," Nick explained to Jim, Ed, Tiny, Marsha and Paddy. "It's really a very simple and sordid case. I thought almost from the very first day I knew who had killed Bill Rinks. I couldn't quite hook it together, though I had all the basics.

"I'm going to gamble that I'm right. I'll take you through every step of this thing, then call a number on the lists. If I'm right, the proof of how it was done will be the answer on that call.

"The thing started back a fairly long time ago, but we're involved in only the past few days, except for the motive. That's from almost twelve years ago. The killer was about to be exposed, or thought she was, as a scheming gold-digging bitch. To be exposed that way would cost her what she'd been working for, in her own way, all her life. She's engaged to marry a disgustingly wealthy old eccentric land developer. He's suspicious and cheap, but he can't live very much longer, even if she has to sort of speed the end.

"That tells you who the killer is. June Cerf.

"There was a detective following her. Her disgustingly wealthy old suitor does *not* trust her, even to the point he demanded a prenuptial agreement. She was about to get that marriage without the agreement, but Bill Rinks knew far too much and she was afraid he'd refuse to hide what he knew from the detective.

"The thing she desperately feared being exposed is that she's mother of an illegitimate child, born eleven years ago. Rinks knew all about it, because the father was the late 'Hands' Bourbonne of New Orleans. Rinks was helping to support the kid from the time it was born. She wasn't. Rinks wasn't going to hide that fact from the private detective Hodgkinson had chasing her.

"If her eccentric millionaire sugar daddy ever learned she'd mothered an illegitimate child he'd probably drop her. If he learned the father was black he *damned* well would! The fact is, she felt Rinks could end her chance to marry tens of millions of dollars.

"She knew about the boat Hodgkinson, or Old Pickle-face, kept in that grass pond because she'd been out there with him in it. The land to the south of that creek for nearly half a mile and back as far belongs to Clearblue Investments, which is owned by Hodgkinson. She also knew the creek went into the gulf. She knew the little channels across the pond. She knew about the trail in there.

"It wasn't hard to set up. She said she'd like to go out for a day to relax and talk or something. She knew the absolutely perfect place! Maybe she said she wanted to make arrangements to take care of her own *dear* little boy once she had all that money, so Rinks agreed to take her out.

"She set up the time, stole the car, and used an aluminum boat and two motors from Gadson's Fish Camp, figured the tide for getting in and out Friday morning, set every-thing up, and got the boat and motors back in time to prevent any great search for them. It was really a simple deal!"

"I can see you've got an answer to how she could appear to be in her office all that time," Paddy said. "Is that what the phone call's about?"

"Uh-huh! That's why she was on the phone out there all the time. Everything's recorded automatically on your phone here, so I'll show exactly how she did it."

"Yeah, but there weren't any calls from her cell phone from out there," Marsha said. "How did you figure that one?"

"There was a number called at three oh three from the canal at Royal Sludge Acres to the same number that three more calls were made later through Everglades City relay station. We were looking at the wrong end of that when we checked the lists.

"Did you notice one of those phones that made the calls from both places was registered to Clearblue Realty Brokers, Inc.?"

"Hodgkinson again!" Jim said. "She could get her hands on any of that stuff she wanted! Anytime!"

"Right! All those calls were made to (He picked up the phone on Paddy's desk and punched the numbers as he said them) five five five four one four seven. Ah!"

He switched on the open speaker. The number rang three times, then, "Miss Cerf is not in the office at the present time. Please leave a message at the tone. If you wish to speak to someone else and are calling from a touch-tone unit, you may now push three for the bar, four for the restaurant, five for the kitchen or six for the maitre D's station ... bleep!"

"Simple. She called her own unlisted number in her own office and punched for whichever place she wanted to raise hell in through the inside system. I could punch four and fire a waitress, three to raise all kinds of hell because of an order of twenty cases instead of two or anything else.

"The important thing is we have four calls to that unlisted number from cell phones out there in the gulf at the times the murderer was seen using a cell phone. No one in the restaurant could tell she wasn't making the calls directly from her office and no one dared to check. We have a complete easy access to who received those calls and when, so we can prove June Cerf made those calls.

"This is tight! If we didn't have one thing other than those calls we could prosecute this one. Details, like motive, are in the back instead of the front. It's been a case that's been more than a little bit weird all along."

"You don't seem to have missed any major details," Paddy said. "I'll get a warrant."

"I couldn't believe that woman!" Al Terns exclaimed after the trial was over and June Cerf was on her way to serving a sentence of life without parole in the Florida State Women's Prison. "I'd met her a few times before and knew her as being self-centered, but not really a bad person. Not so many fool me that way!"

Paddy had been driving the county van they all went to the courthouse in and had offered Al a lift home. They were in Al's back yard, sitting around the wrought iron table, watching the mullet jumping in the canal.

"She was one ice-cold mama," Marsha agreed. "Her own child, Bill Rinks, or nothing else was going to stand in her way to those millions.

"Want to bet Pickleface wouldn't have lived a year if he'd married her?"

"No takers!" Paddy said. "She knew exactly what she wanted. Little things like people were *not* going to slow her down."

"The little lady was brought up being dirt poor," Ed put in. "She was determined to never be poor again, and took it too far. Much too far."

"Are you defending her now?" Nick asked, incredulous.

"Why, no!" Ed replied, the gleam in his eye. "I believe she should have been executed, but I was not on the jury and I was not the judge."

Nick noted the gleam and dropped out of the debate. He saw the amused look on Al's face, and knew he hadn't missed the fact Ed was baiting the bunch of them.

"You just said it was because of the way she was raised!" Jim accused.

"There's no excuse for *any* woman to turn her back on her own child!" Marsha retorted, hotly. "I think they should fry the bitch in hot oil!"

"The judge tried to be fair," Paddy calmed. "He didn't

have such a vicious crime here."

"Have a Collins, now, Nick?" Al asked, holding up a glass.

"Don't mind if I do!"

C. D. Moulton's works are available on most major outlets as printed or e-books. CD writes the CD Grimes, PI, mysteries, the Det. Lt. Nick Storie mysteries, the Clint Faraday mysteries, the Flight of the Maita science fiction series, books on orchid culture and many others of many types. Mystery, adventure, intrigue, science fiction, humor, fantasy, paranormal, mild erotica, and factual.

www.ingramcontent.com/pod-product-compliance
Lightning Source LLC
Chambersburg PA
CBHW052147150726
48002CB00003B/1073